# EVERYTHING HAPPENS AS IT DOES

OPEN LETTER
LITERARY TRANSLATIONS FROM THE UNIVERSITY OF ROCHESTER

# EVERYTHING HAPPENS AS IT DOES

**ALBENA STAMBOLOVA**

Translated from
the Bulgarian
by Olga Nikolova

Library of Congress Cataloging-in-Publication Data: Available.
ISBN-13: 978-1-934824-84-9 / ISBN-10: 1-934824-84-4

This book is published within the Elizabeth Kostova Foundation's
program for Support of Contemporary Bulgarian Writers and in
collaboration with the America for Bulgaria Foundation.

Elizabeth Kostova
FOUNDATION *for*
CREATIVE WRITING

AMERICA FOR BULGARIA
F O U N D A T I O N
Фондация Америка за България

Printed on acid-free paper in the United States of America.

Text set in Dante, a mid-20th-century book typeface designed by Giovanni Mardersteig.
The original type was cut by Charles Malin.

*Design by N. J. Furl*

Open Letter is the University of Rochester's nonprofit, literary translation press:
Lattimore Hall 411, Box 270082, Rochester, NY 14627

www.openletterbooks.org

*All propositions are of equal value. The sense of the world must lie outside the world. In the world everything is as it is, and everything happens as it does happen: in it no value exists—and if it did exist, it would have no value.*

*—Ludwig Wittgenstein;* Tractatus Logico-Philosophicus, 6.41

EVERYTHING HAPPENS AS IT DOES

This story considers itself the story of everyone. I don't know if this is true. You will be the one to decide.

I myself am certain that all stories are love stories, so I have refrained from classifying it as such.

It is simply the story of women and men who are mothers and fathers, sisters and brothers, loved ones and friends . . . or, in a nutshell, of people who are tigers and lions, oranges and lemons.

This story is neither funny, nor sad. It is simply a story that takes place somewhere on the border between the world we know and the world we are no longer very sure about.

## 1.
## *Little Boys and Their Parents*

In the beginning, Boris was unable to think about the surrounding world. Things just happened to him, and he had no way of avoiding them.

His parents, for example, meek as they were, looked like a grandpa and a grandma rather than a mother and a father, and that always unsettled him. His sister was eighteen years older than him, and people mistook her for his mother.

Later, as he grew older, he devised a way to escape. He would try to lose himself in uninhabited worlds, where it was hard to establish relationships of the family kind.

It was with the bees that he first managed to draw the boundaries of something he could call his own.

Before he enrolled in the English Language School in Plovdiv, he had a lot of time on his hands and nothing to do. He made it his purpose simply to pass the time. Afterward the opposite happened: he learned to stretch time to fit whatever work he was doing. And to stay in his room, while his sister's family, although he was supposed to be living with them, carried on a life of its own.

When he started wearing glasses, the painful awkwardness of his childish face shifted into a look of seriousness. The glasses somehow set everyone at ease, as if things had finally slipped into place. Wearing glasses had the effect of calming the vague fears the family harbored about Boris. Not that they now knew him better than before. But an introverted boy with glasses was less worrisome than an introverted boy without glasses.

Boris could feel the change in people's perception of him and immediately saw its advantages. Later, when he grew a beard, he could see how, just as the glasses before, the beard replaced whatever it was in him that provoked fear in others. One thing substituted for another. And behind it all stood the child named Boris.

He never asked himself how others did it. Getting to an inviolable place of his own was all that mattered, and he could always tell when he was there.

He learned to do things no one paid attention to. Or to do things in such a way that no one paid attention to him. For instance, he was willing to eat something he couldn't stand, rather than give himself away and make his dislike known to others. He realized that his mother felt anxiety and, although he could not understand why, he felt he knew enough already.

## 2.
## *Christening*

Then the eight-year-old grandson of the old woman died. She lived in the neighboring house and the boy used to spend the summers with her. His father and mother would drive him there in June; they would visit him, bringing some food, several times in July and August, and finally they would come and take him back for school in September. Boris and the boy were the same age and knew each other vaguely. But since Boris never played with other children, the city boy had more friends than he did.

Fishing occupied the boys' time in the summer. The reservoir was thick with ooze and stale water but generations of carp lived in it. Boris could tell where the boys gathered by the smoke columns of their fires. The air smelled of dry timber and food. Or rather, of what they called "food"—their catch. Boris did not want to have anything to do with them. Neither the boys, nor the fish, nor what the boys did with the fish, appealed to him.

Nobody could explain how the city boy drowned. One evening he just didn't come home to his grandmother.

Grief settled like a cloud over the entire summer. Boris's mother took him to see the boy. Even later, as an adult, he still couldn't understand why the child was dressed in white and laid in a flower-covered coffin, by which everyone in the village stopped to bow.

When Boris left a flower inside the coffin, as his mother had instructed him, he felt like this was a kind of punishment. People wailed over the boy's death as if they had killed him themselves.

It was the first time Boris had seen a dead person. A child. He stared at the calm face and suddenly thought that the boy had managed to hide somewhere. He was pierced by jealousy, wishing he, too, could become invisible to others.

As usual, he never mentioned a word about this to anyone.

For the rest of the summer, the children were not seen in their playing grounds. The weather became unbearably hot. Storms rose every now and again, blowing down twigs and leaves. The old woman stayed in her house. Sent by his mother, Boris would occasionally bring soup and bread to her. The old woman would sit or lie in a small heap on the floor. All the doors would be open. But all the windows closed.

Boris liked visiting her. She didn't look at him or speak to him. He never caught her sleeping. Whenever he entered, he noticed her opened eyes first. She looked past him into the distance. Her eyes were beautiful, Boris thought. Full of attention and smiling. She never appeared confused or scared.

He would leave another bowl and a piece of bread wrapped in cloth on the table, taking the old ones. The woman never touched them. Boris would then sit on the edge of the bed, chasing away the flies. For some reason the kitchen was much cooler than the rest of the house. Or it just seemed so to him. The old woman had also found a way to hide herself, and Boris wanted to know how. He felt good sitting with her, even better than with his bees. It was difficult to leave. Once, his mother came looking for him. He saw her coming into the garden and got up to meet her. If she had seen him sitting on the bed with the old woman, he would have felt ashamed. To sit with her was something that only belonged to him and he did not want his mother to know about it. He rushed outside, and his mother stayed in the house for quite a while.

---

## 3.

## *Farther Up*

---

At the end of that summer, his parents decided to baptize him. God only knows why they hadn't done it earlier. Boris was mortified. He could not understand why this had to happen to him: it never happened to anyone else. The comparison caught him unprepared; he was not used to seeing his life measured up against those of others. He was overcome by panic at the prospect of this mystery in which he was to become the main protagonist. But he understood that he would be doing something for his parents, something, whatever it was, for their benefit.

He let them dress him in clothes he had never seen before and joined the procession of adults on the forest path leading to the chapel. They forbade him to carry anything with him. He felt content moving along the path, observing how his feet followed each other over the ground. One foot, the other foot, then again, as if moving by their own volition.

Movement and silence hand in hand. Intimations of other silences, of other movements, of someone walking next to someone, hovered around them. Each bend in the path made him anticipate the next. It was anticipation too brief to invite fear, under the dome of the indefinite woods, dimensionless like a house never visited.

Everything required silence. Stepping was almost like walking. Yet not quite. He discovered that stepping on the path was a cautious pleasure, felt by him and felt by others, a shared pleasure. They stepped side by side and moved toward the next bend, a little farther up the slope, hand in hand with that silence.

Boris and the others. It was possible as long as there was silence. Together in the half-light of the dome. The place opened up to receive the procession.

And Boris learned that the world could be this way. No one was rude. No one touched anyone in the increasingly dense stillness, which had now become a permeable environment. Behind them, he could hear a rustling sound like that of a snake's tail among the thickening layer of rust-colored leaves. There was no need to turn back to look. Before them lay the same full-bodied stream of leaves, from all these different years, and his feet sank in them to his ankles. Many autumns under their feet, their feet now invisible, driving them down the same path, along the same steps, already made by others. Where others had walked. Years later, Margarita would try to explain a similar thing about her grandmother's lamp and only Boris, to an extent, would be able to understand her.

He pictured the chapel from time to time. He had no idea how far it was. Or if it was white or if it was small.

They stepped on the leaves and were silent. In their silence was nothing they wished to conceal.

Boris began to love this walk, just as he had begun to love the old woman.

The steps followed one another, alone, together, sometimes simultaneously, not according to any rule. But the steps were not made, they were making themselves. The walking did the walking itself and he was there, knowing the chapel was at the end of the road. A place in this big house where they found themselves together.

Then he saw it. He was already in front of the door, almost as big as the chapel itself. They told him to open it.

Boris pushed the door with the tips of his fingers and it opened beautifully, revealing in the coming light a small space where someone was sitting. A tiny woman in black, whose eyes he was to meet again years later. Eyes the color of fog. He drew back his fingers and the door gently closed.

---

## 4.
## *Bees and Their Friends*

---

Boris cohabited with bees; bees cohabited with him. The very first time his father took him to the beehive not too far from the house, the bees and Boris immediately took to each other. He was interested in the way his father pulled the honeycomb frames and pushed them back like drawers. They made the same sound. It all seemed like a game to his childish eyes.

Later his father would say that the bees did not gather around him, but swarmed around Boris. His father's head was covered with a net, propped from below by a wide-brimmed hat. The shape of a planet. But Boris would learn this only later, in school. That there were celestial bodies, spheres, some of them with rings. Saturn. His father's head at the beehive was like Saturn. Boris liked Saturn very much.

Later, when Maria read ancient Greek myths to him, he learned that Saturn was the father of Jupiter. Or rather, that Chronos was the father of Zeus. Saturn and Jupiter were their Latin names.

Maria had become his wife by then. But at the beehive he had no idea she even existed.

After that first time, Boris regularly went with his father to see the bees. He did not like the taste of honey. Perhaps that was why the bees liked him. He ate honey sometimes, because he had to comply with his mother's wishes, but he never enjoyed it. He knew from the very beginning that honey belonged to the bees, and his father rattling the drawers now seemed silly.

When he found a wild beehive for the first time, he saw how imperfect the man-made beehives were, with their little toy roofs. Doll houses in which the bees were forced to do what they naturally did anyway. Such things, and others, would cross his mind.

At some point he learned that there were queen bees, drones, and brood chambers, and this filled him with admiration. The worker-bees worked; they did their tasks without thinking. Boris decided that human beings were imperfect in comparison, because they would always think while doing things. And they would tire— whereas bees never grew tired. They simply reacted to changes in temperature. They stopped being bees below such-and-such degrees.

He gathered honey, filling jars with amber. Other people in the village also had beehives, but Boris seemed to have a special gift; he was so good at it that everyone relished his honey.

He never put on a beekeeper's veil. Not a single bee ever bothered or stung him. Boris found bees to be perfect and tried to learn everything there was to learn about them. Then he became the bees' man. And they became Boris's bees.

Year in, year out, the same thing would happen. Boris would lie down in the tall, soft grass between the beehives. At first he would hear them moving along their flight paths, then a wave of information signals that he could clearly sense would traverse the air. The bees would start hovering above him, and he knew that they were trying to decide which ones should descend on him. They would begin to land on him, covering first the bare skin, his hands and face, and afterward his entire body. They would stay there until he stirred to get up. Then they would lift off at once like a cloud of sound and he would walk away. He would eventually leave them behind and they would again busy themselves about their bee work.

No one knew that Boris and the bees had a special relationship. Or perhaps no one wished to know. The bees, just as the glasses did later, provided enough explanation for the boy's absentminded wandering, his reticence and his lack of interest in the food on his plate.

## 5.
## Sisters and Brothers

His reticence did not diminish with the years. Since he learned faster than others, he had the small privilege of taking his exams in writing. They had suggested to his parents that he should pass some tests and go to a school for gifted children. But his parents had rejected the idea. What difference did it make if the child could learn faster—sending Boris to a different school meant acknowledging he was different. And that would have been too much.

But when he ranked first in the entry exams for the English Language School, there was no choice. Boris was to live with his sister in Plovdiv, where his room had already been prepared.

He didn't feel like leaving the village. Here he had conquered his own territory and he knew he could be left alone. In the city, he would have to start from scratch.

In any case, he had no choice. He had to continue his studies. He was glad he was older, because with age, the opportunities to raise barriers between himself and others grew larger.

His life in Plovdiv began with observing his sister's family. A husband and two children; he was the children's uncle. They all behaved as if being a family was the most natural thing in the world. The family seemed to engender and maintain itself. Maybe that was the case.

He quickly managed to discourage his sister from accompanying him anywhere. He drew his own itineraries and came to like the city, where he could be even less visible.

He liked the open-air amphitheater the best. There were people there at all times, like everywhere else in the city, but the space was designed for it. It was created with many people in mind. Even when it was empty, a distant din seemed to ripple through the air, inhabiting the area. He was moved by this ghostly presence. To him the human race appeared remarkable, as long as it remained at a distance.

The idea of apartment space, for example, seemed ridiculous to him. In the kitchen you cook. In the sitting room you sit. The bedroom is for sleep, and the children's room is for play. And in order to legitimize this division of space, people fitted each room with the respective pieces of furniture and appliances. And as if that was not enough, the damn shapes of these spaces simply drove him to despair.

They were all the same. He could see it from the outside. A mere glimpse at the façade and he could picture the hive inside. A hive that was not a real hive, and was much worse than the little man-made toy houses for the so-called domestic bees. What human beings considered rational was miles away from the living economy of bees. Between the act of pressing the washing machine button and the mood of the person pressing it there was an entire universe of folly that people called their lives.

Houses were a different story—when they were not ruined by the desire to transform them into modern apartments. They revealed unexpected spaces, which welcomed human beings the way a wooded glade did. But that was rare. He had looked carefully at all the houses in the old part of the city, but they all resembled taxidermied animals. Even if they had been alive before, today they were lifeless. Their colors were almost painful to look at.

His sister made it her habit to come into his room to wake him early in the morning. Even when she realized that Boris was always awake by the time she came in, she persisted. He decided not to deprive her of this privilege, allowing her to keep this tiny harmless territory so he could gain much larger terrain. For example, the right to be absent from the evening gatherings of the family. Or the right not to watch television.

His sister began to feel a peculiar awe toward him. Once Boris had openly acknowledged that he was different, she was no longer surprised by anything he did. He functioned like clockwork, always doing the same things at the same time of day, without showing impatience or boredom. He never talked about school or about his friends. How was he?—He was fine. Was everything alright?—It was.

The profound difference between them was compensated for by the absence of any serious problems. His behavior suggested that everything was under control, and people around him, at a loss about what else to think, reassured themselves that indeed "everything was under control," believing they had reached that conclusion alone. Meanwhile, Boris spent his time reading, the overlap between his inner and outer age thinned, and he seemed to be always deep in thought, always thinking, but about what—that was beyond anyone's guess.

6.
## Ghosts

Something did happen once, however. Or, to put it differently, something went out of control once.

Because of his calmness, Boris could often join a small group of classmates walking together part of the way back from school. Since he could accommodate both their conversation and his own thoughts, his classmates, tame enough, accepted his silent presence. He nodded, replied in monosyllables, and smiled if necessary so they would not consider him a complete stranger. Besides, for some inexplicable reason, he looked like an athlete; he was as fit as other boys would be only with much exercise. One day he took part in a group fight and that, once and for all, confirmed his right to be there, doing nothing.

There was a girl in the group who, despite his resistance, drew his attention. He could not explain the phenomenon in any rational way. The girl wore a pleated skirt, spread out like an umbrella over legs as thin as walking sticks, and that was that. Boris never looked at her, but was somehow constantly aware of her position or movement, which he felt like a spatial relation he could not overcome. He rebelled against this awareness which was forcing itself upon him, mobilized all his strength to destroy it, but it remained intact, as if some part of his mind, insusceptible to reason, kept registering the girl's presence. Perpetual motion. She was there, she was not there, she was approaching, she was moving away, tick-tick-tick—the skirt with the little legs.

His record of warmth-waves expanded like a file. The information, most of it monotonous and unvaried, kept accumulating, and Boris felt he now lived with it, as if it was his second heart.

A year passed, and then another. The girl stopped wearing the umbrella skirt, but he never even noticed. He was collecting the data of her movements, her appearances and disappearances. An oscillogram. Until one day she vanished from his life.

Late one evening, having wandered through the streets for a while, he saw her walking up the front of a white house. With her skirt and her thin little legs. Like a fly, like a bee. He saw her and that was that. He blinked in the moonlight, but he still saw her. She climbed to the eaves and continued over the roof, reached its top and disappeared on the other side.

Boris stood motionless in the silence. It never crossed his mind to run to the other side and watch her descent. He knew she was climbing down the other side. And so he left, carrying with him the image of the girl walking down the back wall of a white house.

---

## 7.
## Digital Worlds

---

He kept reading until the moment he discovered computers. Then he finally entered a world that corresponded to his own expectations—he found a new way of creating order. A new way of possessing what he called his own. Entrances were designated by icons.

There was nothing friendlier in his life than these icons, behind which sparkled his treasures. The icons multiplied, and the electronic beeps with which his computer responded felt closer to home than anything else.

Then he began to create virtual civilizations. Primitive, medieval, improbable, all kinds of civilizations. Their populations grew according to the variables he would input, and people slaughtered each other, they always destroyed themselves completely, whether their lives were short, or long. The civilizations that quickly declined were not his favorites. He learned how to keep an archive of their histories and return to it for reference. Gradually he began to see the mistakes he had made, if these could indeed be called mistakes. He was not using all available options.

His first virtual worlds were short-lived, like explosions. Later they began to resemble pyramids, then spirals. The graphs of their development showed their respective level of stability. His goal was to create a kaleidoscopic civilization. He tried setting aleatory parameters. But his creations did not submit to such operations.

Then he started to feel some kind of responsibility for the people in his virtual worlds. And fear. Their longevity and their death depended on him. At first he liked the idea, but then he began to feel uncomfortable. Events were taking place on his computer even in his absence. Whenever he peeked inside, he was astounded to see how much his creations had progressed. He began to realize that his task was to slow down their development. And slowing it down meant adding more parameters. This, in turn, meant more variables. He searched for an optimal relationship between input parameters and the predictability of outcomes.

And, at some point, toward the end of high school, he knew what he wanted to do later in life.

---

8.
## Fathers and Their Professions

---

Philip met Maria at a friend's house. Although he never liked to admit it, he failed to notice her at first. She had been sitting in some part of the room, watching him. He had felt her gaze, though without being able to identify where it came from.

For a long time afterward, he wondered why this creature stood there draped in black cloth, as if she were an extra in a bustling film scene.

Philip was a pathologist, and that caused him both annoyance and relief. He was the only one among his friends who could say in a word what he did for a living. For a twenty-seven-year-old man it made things easier. But when people, curious about the nature of his work, started asking questions, he was not good at explaining.

The voice on the phone had moved him so unexpectedly and profoundly that he had nearly hung up. He couldn't remember what they said to each other, just as later he couldn't recall anything specific from conversations with Maria. But he could remember situations in which her presence or her voice obliterated everything else.

It was impossible to say "no" to this voice, which was now calling to him from the receiver. Why him, and not someone else, he never understood. Here I am, Lord.

He proposed to her almost immediately, not knowing what he was doing. He knew only that he could not have done otherwise. She nodded, as if she had foreseen long ago that this was bound to happen.

Time seemed to be out of joint. The days were shamelessly short, the nights blended into one. Something was ripening in Philip; he could feel it in nervous spasms, but ignored it. He was spinning with Maria in a whirlwind. He had turned into a boomerang, always meekly landing at her feet, no matter what he thought, no matter what he did, and no matter who he saw.

Before meeting Maria, he had been simply Philip, a doctor, a pathologist. He had been able to describe himself in a word.

After meeting Maria, his center of gravity was transposed out of his body, and in the beginning this gave him strength. Strength that Maria absorbed.

# 9

# The Hero's Prize

There was no wedding. They merely signed a marriage certificate. She never allowed him to see her passport. The civil servant was allowed to see it, but not her husband. He had no idea when she was born, or who her parents were, or whether she had any siblings. Whenever he asked her about these things, she laughed, as if his questions were the most inappropriate thing in the world. He was surprised to discover how easy it was to lie to his friends or family when they asked the same questions. And he deluded himself that one day he would surely find out, as soon as Maria stopped playing this funny game. Then he forgot about it and remembered it again only when it was too late.

She did not simply give herself to him—she laid herself out like a gift, like an offering. He sank into her with the feeling that he had never experienced anything like this before. All thoughts and questions vanished. Maria became a world he inhabited. He knew he must have done things, at least he must have eaten food and drunk water. Later, when the doctor asked him, he could not remember anything, only that he had felt tireless and strong.

She stayed at home knitting sweaters. There was always a cooked meal to eat. Maria always had money and the food was always tasty. So tasty that, after dinner, his only wish was to take her in his arms and bury his face in her long hair.

She became pregnant almost by magic. Philip was certain it had happened the very first time. If happiness meant being able to stop thinking, Philip was happy. Things just happened and he was part of the process.

The twins were born. A boy, Valentin, and a girl, Margarita. Philip didn't recall ever discussing what names to choose. It seemed like they were born with their names.

## 10.
## *After the Fairy Tale's End*

Then he became frightened of Maria.

One night, he woke up and looked at his sleeping wife. He watched her for a long time. He was certain that she was not asleep. She lay perfectly still, as if absent from her body.

For the first time he wondered whether a human being had a beginning and an end. He looked at her. Maria was sleeping naked, covered by her hair as if with a blanket. Her breath was barely perceptible. No adjectives could describe her for him. He couldn't say that she was kind, for example, or anything like that. This creature had simply appeared and in the face of this fact Philip was powerless. He was overcome with despair. What were his, or her feelings? Only the dispersing of stardust.

Suddenly, he realized that Maria was staring at him. Perhaps everyone who has just risen from sleep had this look in their eyes. Maria's look was evil. At last, something definite. Philip had come to know something and now he could see she did not like it. Her eyes stared unblinkingly, as if she had no eyelids.

He got up from the bed and left the room.

After this first onrush of fear, Philip tried to talk to his brother.

His brother told him that Maria was breaking all accepted codes of behavior.

At first he did not understand what this meant. Gradually, it dawned on him that his brother was accusing him of being disloyal. Toward himself, toward his family, and his friends. The sound of these trivial words, which he hadn't heard pronounced for a while, unsettled him.

That same night, Maria refused to sleep with him, and he knew her refusal was going to last.

Philip tried to lose himself in his work. From then on, he often slept at the hospital, he worked night shifts, and became better at his job. He was called in more often for criminal cases. He discovered courtrooms.

But he also started drinking. And drinking brought back his ability to speak.

## 11.
## The Twins

Valentin's anger toward his sister was boundless. She was the same as him and she was different. He felt ashamed to have a sister. He invented and did all kinds of things, and she just sat there, dull, watching him. He did not want this lump, so similar to him, to sit there and watch him. He did not want to have a sister.

When they began school, his mother was no longer there to take his sister in her arms whenever she started weeping. It quickly became clear that Margarita could not stay in the same school. This solved the problem, and after rejecting the idea for a year, his mother agreed to send her to another school, for children like her. Although no one knew exactly what his sister was like. Except perhaps his mother, but she never said anything.

Margarita thus disappeared from Valentin's life. At least for a while. She reappeared during weekends, but he had other things to do, he had friends, and his mother would simply take her out somewhere.

He could remember how his father once became very angry about Maria and Margarita's going out. He had insisted on joining them, he had insisted on being told what they intended to do together. Maria had ignored his shouting. When the two women were ready to leave, his mother whispered something in his sister's ear, and Margarita remained by the door to wait. His mother then went into the bedroom with his father.

After that everything quieted down, as if someone had enclosed the world in a box. The two children fixed the bedroom door with their eyes. Valentin looked at Margarita. A peculiar thought crossed his mind, but by then his mother had reappeared. Without a word, she grabbed Margarita's hand and they went out.

Valentin waited for a while, then gently opened the bedroom door. His father was snoring happily in his bed.

When they brought the piano to the house, his mother said it was for Margarita. Valentin could not believe it—such a big and important object meant for this miserable, annoying little thing that was his sister.

In the beginning, Maria herself taught Margarita how to play. Valentin discovered that his mother could play the piano. He felt extremely proud and wanted to learn to play too. But she would not have it, the piano was for Margarita.

He remembered that later a blond woman would come to the house and play the piano with Margarita.

Then Margarita started playing the piano by herself and Valentin lost interest in the whole affair. One day, after many years, when they were about fifteen years old, a friend of his happened to hear Margarita play and said he wanted to see her. They tiptoed into the dusky living room and listened to her unnoticed for a long time. When she stopped, she saw them and ran away into her room.

His friend, however, who was the son of musicians, could not leave it alone. He wanted to see the sheet music, he wanted to know if Margarita studied at a music school . . . They searched for the sheet music everywhere, but found nothing. The boy insisted that what they had heard was the finale of a very special sonata by César Franck, which people studied for the entry exams of the Conservatoire. And that Margarita played it like a virtuoso.

## 12.
## Raya

Valentin thought that Raya was an incredible woman.

Her family was everything his family was not. Grandmothers and grandfathers from all different branches of the family tree kept appearing, either in person or on portraits hung on walls.

In this open and overpopulated house, Raya chirped like God's little bird.

The house echoed with laughter and music. The radio boomed and piles of newspapers and magazines lay under armchairs or right in the middle of rooms.

Valentin, like all other visitors, was welcomed as part of the house. In this house, children, both the family's and other people's, played hide-and-seek and blind man's bluff, they knocked over half-empty tea cups and threw stray newspapers in crumpled balls. Beautiful little pictures surprised one in unexpected corners. But the chaos was not at all filthy or shabby; it was the receptacle for the peculiar life of this incomprehensible and wonderful house, which attracted Valentin like a magnet.

Raya was not so much the child of her parents as an offspring of the house and the life in it. To win Raya meant to be accepted by the house. Whether Valentin and Raya were in love, whether they slept together—such things passed unquestioned in the general state of absent-mindedness. No one, neither the children, nor the adults, were interested in such details.

From the very beginning, Valentin realized that being part of the family came first, and being with Raya came second. Perhaps that was why he didn't take any precautions—it was the desire to leave a trace, to win a place for himself in the group picture. Gradually he began to feel anxious, realizing that he was after something which was only important to him, but not anyone else. Not to Raya, and not to the rest of them.

Little by little, the foreboding that it was all doomed overpowered him. He could no longer fight it. And no one around him seemed to notice anything. The sisters, the cousins and the little brothers, the grandfathers and the aunts, the parents and their parents, no one seemed to suspect for even a moment that Valentin, once having formed a part of this harmony, could ever break away from it.

Valentin was nearing a steep ledge. He felt neglected. Raya could not understand why he felt this way. But he blundered on, trying to step outside the family circle. A game of blind man's bluff of a different nature. He adored Raya for her inimitable ease: she did not have to try to be this way or that way, she did not need to make decisions and stick to them, she did not need directions. But he also hated her for it and wanted to destroy that in her.

The rupture came when she got pregnant. Everyone felt betrayed. The endless joyride was over. Valentin knew that, in this household, everyone loved everyone else and did what was best for them. The best for Raya was to preserve her childhood; the best for the pregnant Raya was to marry Valentin, but leaving the house was out of the question. Valentin had slept with her, but she was a child of the clan, her baby would be a child of the clan, and so Valentin was invited to become the same.

He closed his eyes and tried to picture it. After a brief silence, the Ferris wheel turns again for another ride. One more sweet little baby crawls on the floor, vomits over the rich thick carpet, and everyone laughs. Raya's older brother hugs the baby as if it were his own, her younger brother plays with him as if it were his baby brother, her father throws a bemused look, not sure whether the tiny creature is his grandson, or some kind of great grand-nephew, or even—why not—his own son. At this point in his imaginative reconstruction, the water in Valentin's body reached boiling.

After that, Valentin could not hold back from acting stupidly. He knew he was destroying everything, and this time it was not because he wanted something else. Raya cried at his wickedness. And she became increasingly miserable, because she could not understand where it was all coming from. He himself could barely understand what he was doing, yet he felt that it was his turn to act. He was obsessed by the idea that part of Raya belonged to him and he wouldn't share that part with anyone. Within the communal Garden of Eden of her family, his behavior appeared disgusting. So be it, then—he was disgusting.

He lay down impossible conditions and made demands he knew Raya could not satisfy. For instance, he wanted them to live separately, just the two of them. There were strong arguments against it—they could not support themselves. They were still in school. They were too young. But why couldn't they get jobs and be like a normal family? Raya did not understand the meaning of "normal family." She imagined work as some kind of hobby that had nothing to do with earning money. And she imagined herself as a molecule of some precious substance whose chemical formula was her family's secret.

Then Valentin disappeared. He disappeared from their life together, from the life of his baby, and from his own life, which had only just begun to acquire a life-like shape.

Or, to be more precise, he tried to disappear, going back to the house he had always inhabited—the house of his mother.

## 13.
## Maria's Baby

It was then that he discovered that his mother was also expecting a baby. And that a new protagonist, named Boris, had appeared on the scene.

Boris had already moved into his mother's house. At first Valentin was resentful. His father was God knows where, behaving like a madman, and here was this new person with his glasses, only a couple of years older than himself, who barely even spoke a word. His mother and Margarita were not very generous in their explanations, either—Boris was a molecular biologist of international reputation, a genius in his domain, a vagabond wiseacre who had, however, ended up here with his two enormous black suitcases. Whatever Valentin had hoped for in his attempt to disappear, there was no empty wilderness to be found here. There was a new storyline just beginning to emerge.

Although it seemed somehow absurd, Valentin told his mother, more or less, about Raya and her baby. Maria immediately said that they were welcome to come here, the three of them, or the two of them, whatever they decided. Curiously, though, she did not say a word about the possibility of his coming to stay here alone. Valentin wondered for a while if this was supposed to mean anything, then let it be, deciding that the whole thing was too complicated. Yet he felt like a ship stuck on a reef. In escaping one all-devouring organism, he had landed in the hands of another.

On the other hand, given that Maria almost never left the house: how had she and Boris gotten to know each other?

The subject of marriage was breached only after Maria met Boris's parents.

The old man and the old woman in their little house were like characters from a fairy tale.

When Boris brought Maria to meet them, they could hardly see her face beyond her enormous belly. She could not bend much, so she simply sat on the floor at their feet in order to kiss their hands. Her hair spread around her like a cloak.

Boris had never seen Maria's eyes so clear. They were usually murky, like fog, but now they had a gray opal-like shimmer that was new to him. The expression in her eyes was also new to him. Maria looked at the old man and the old woman as if she had just recognized in them her long lost parents.

Boris left them and walked up the path to the chapel. It was the first time he had returned there since his christening. Since he had pushed the big door with his fingers and had seen, sitting inside the chapel, a tiny woman with eyes like fog.

This time there was no one inside. He walked in and sat on the floor opposite the door, which slowly closed before him. He sat down exactly on the spot where he had seen her. The moment his back touched the wall, he suddenly felt that he was her. That he was she, and she was that woman, and he was the baby she was carrying and she was his parents in their little house down the hill. There was a soft hum in the chapel that made him drowsy. He sat there for a while, or maybe it was just a minute. Sitting was timeless. He recalled the gaze of the dead boy's grandmother, he heard his own hands chasing off the flies, he saw the little ballet dancer climbing down the wall, he became one with Maria, joined in holy matrimony.

When he came back to the house, everyone was asleep. He wished things could stay this way forever. Halcyon silence dripped from the trees. He felt strong like never before. The missing link with his parents was finally found. He could be their son, now that Maria was here.

One evening Margarita tripped over two enormous suitcases lying in the dark hallway. She knew immediately why they were there. She knew that what had happened to her father, and later to Valentin, was now happening to Boris.

It was his turn to leave. Nothing could be done to prevent it. Maria had made up her mind.

Margarita could vaguely sense that she was the only one with any influence over her mother. But she had no idea what she could do.

Boris was not in the house. The suitcases were there, but he was gone. Her mother had also gone somewhere. Margarita decided to open the suitcases. She reached for one of them.

The metal locks were lovely; they were cold and made a clicking sound. She lifted the lid and, pushing it back, propped it against the wall and blocked the entire hallway. There were no clothes in the suitcase, only books, folders, floppy disks and various little devices with a mysterious purpose. They were so small and shiny; she liked them very much. She was not sure what one was supposed to do with them. Just look. Then what? Margarita pressed a button and heard a voice. Boris's voice saying things she couldn't understand. She kept listening to the recording and played the whole thing. Boris barely ever spoke, yet here, in the dark hallway, his voice seemed to have a life of its own. Boris and the voice of Boris were separate. Margarita was not surprised, it seemed natural to her. She found a box full of tapes and began to play them one by one. When she started to feel cold, she got into the suitcase, where the hard objects made room for her. She nestled cozily, listening to the fairy tales of the voice from the little machine. Boris was good at telling stories. Margarita could see that right away. This Boris from the machine was a different Boris that no one had heard speak before and no one had ever met. These stories were meant for nobody, or maybe nobody and Margarita. It didn't occur to her to ask why Boris was telling them. She just followed his voice in this exciting adventure, and there was suspense and something important was about to happen; things were becoming more and more interesting, and she fell asleep just before what seemed to be some kind of beginning. The lid of the suitcase closed itself gently, so as not to wake her, and in the darkness inside, Boris's voice went on speaking.

## 15.
## Revelations

The sweaters Maria knitted for her men never left the house for good.

They would leave for a while on someone's back, then they would return to be washed or mended, and they would leave again, not necessarily on the same shoulders.

Margarita remembered what had happened with her father. In the beginning, like a guest in a boarding house, Philip would have only dinner with them. Maria would retire to bed early and he would stay alone with the twins for hours. He would come and go with bags full of clothes. He would always change, never leaving with the same clothes in which he arrived.

They would sit at the table and Philip would talk about his work. Valentin would try to appear interested, but Margarita would simply stare absently, as usual. Her father was here and that was enough. At some point Philip and Valentin would grow bored. But not Margarita, because she never took part in any of the conversation. Valentin would excuse himself, saying he had to wake up early, and Philip would feel confused. Had he left them already? He wasn't sure. He couldn't explain why he no longer slept at home. The many glasses of wine he drank made him talkative at first, but then he became withdrawn, as if descending into something, some place to which Margarita often tried to find entry. They would sit with this nothingness between them, so dense and heavy that it forced them to turn inward and search for something inside, each searching alone.

Philip would walk with Margarita to her room, then go about doing whatever he was doing. They let him wander around the house like a ghost. And he probably did wander like a ghost. By morning he was always gone.

He would leave behind clothes strewn here and there around the rooms. Maria would carefully pick them up, and wash and iron them. That was all. Their father was a pile of clothes Maria took care of. He would happen to appear inside these clothes for a brief moment during his increasingly rare visits, and that was it. The twins began to perceive his presence as fortuitous, feeling that they knew him less and less. Then their father started wearing unfamiliar clothes, which he no longer left in the house, until, finally, the thread connecting all of these things became so thin that when she saw Maria knitting another sweater, Margarita asked her who it was for.

Her mother looked at her without saying anything, as she always did, and looked at her for so long that Margarita realized the answer was irrelevant. Anyone could wear this sweater, even her father—who was wearing it, who had worn it before, who would wear it after, for how long—none of these made any difference to the sweater itself.

## 16.
## *Spiders and Their Webs*

There is marvel in the world. Nobody has taught us how to marvel, and that is why no one knows what marvel is.

To look from the inside out and from the outside in are two different things.

Margarita bumped into walls all the time. It hurt. But Margarita knew how to stare at a thing long enough to obliterate the difference between inside and out.

She would often hide, for example, in the spider's web in the corner of her room.

Her favorite spider. From here the filaments and threads looked like a thicket. A thicket full of glimmer.

Valentin would be raging down there, furiously shaking what he believed to be Margarita, and she would be swinging on the filaments up here, laughing.

# 17.
## *Margarita*

Margarita was unable to concentrate on anything. She was prover-
bially absentminded—these were the words people used to describe
her. The moment she managed to focus on something, she was
frightened by what she saw. She preferred to float around things
rather than see them. Besides, she rarely felt she was in any danger.

Margarita's brain clicked like a camera shutter. She would close
her eyes and when she opened them again, the world would be
different. People lived in this world, and she lived with them. She
was like an amiable, myopic insect.

However, she was now old enough to know a few things. There
were rules for dealing with people. Rules meant to make sure she
didn't scare anyone. Simple rules.

She had realized long ago that she frightened her father. She did
her best to avoid causing him worry. She tried hard to behave the
way he expected her to. But that was as far as it went. Margarita
was, after all, Margarita, and even her father would never be able
to understand her.

Most of the time she played the piano for him. Music brought
back something in him, something he loved but could not reach in
any other way. When his daughter played the piano, Philip admired
her ability to remember scores. But soon enough he would forget
about the scores and surrender to the music—the way, he remembered, he had surrendered to Maria.

He was aware that something inappropriate was taking place. It
was huge and it was not supposed to happen.

Margarita would always sense when the current would start trickling out of her father. As if Philip's surface had cracked. She would stop playing then. It was her way of showing her love.

Then he would shut down and leave. She had no idea why.

Her relationship with her brother had improved. Now he was a student at the university and he was telling her about all kinds of things. Margarita listened to him in her typical manner—she would concentrate for a second, following the story, then she would lose the thread again. Valentin would react in a funny way—he would get angry, as if Margarita was deliberately trying to annoy him. "She can't understand a word. I'm just wasting my time." Then he would come back, astonished by how much she actually remembered. And who said she needed to understand everything?

He would sometimes study for his exams with her and then they had a lot of fun. She knew she was helping him and felt proud.

Gradually, having the experience of other relationships, Valentin became very attached to his sister. Margarita was like a crystal mirror. Also, she was becoming prettier by the day. Her beauty had something childish and fragile about it. It was incredibly easy to hurt her or make her anxious.

According to Valentin, their mother was giving them too much freedom. A helpless creature like Margarita, who could get into all kinds of trouble, being out and about doing God knows what . . . He couldn't bear the thought. But as usual, when he finally summoned the courage to speak to Maria, their conversation just dissipated into smiles and looks, which made Valentin realize that nothing would change, that he was worrying for no reason, and nothing bad could ever happen to Margarita.

After that conversation, he started taking Margarita with him whenever he could. He became closer to people who showed an attitude toward her similar to his own. In various circles of friends, Margarita was thus welcomed and loved. It became easier for Valentin to know where she went when she went alone. Sooner or later someone would tell him they saw her somewhere. Or he would try to guess.

Their relationship with Maria was odd. Maria had never seemed worried that one of the twins was different. In fact, around her mother, Margarita was at her most normal. Maria allowed her things that were forbidden to others—for example, she allowed her to come to her, avoiding the girl much less than she avoided everyone else; she even went to Margarita herself; she let her cuddle and play with her hair. Maria would always read fairy tales to her and Margarita knew them by heart. Margarita knew count-less fairy tales. When she learned how to read, only Maria showed no surprise. But she did not appear happy about it either. As if the fact that Margarita was gradually entering the world of other people destroyed some essential bond with her mother. Valentin had noticed that his sister was a little timid with their mother, afraid to let her know that the world had become bigger, or that it had left any permanent traces in her mind.

Maria did not protest when Valentin started taking his sister out. But he knew that she didn't like it and was merely tolerating it for the time being.

## 18.
## Girls and Mirrors

No matter what she put on, the mirror reflected back an unfamiliar image.

In the beginning this seemed normal. One put on clothes in order to become someone else. Changing clothes changed everything.

But there was also what she could observe in other people. For example, her mother. For a very long time she believed that Maria always wore the same clothes. Her mother was her mother and that was it. When she began to notice that Maria's clothes were similar, yet different from one day to the next, she went to the bedroom and opened the wardrobe. It was filled with darkness—all clothes were dark-colored, most of them black, and all of them shapeless, masses of fabric with an occasional seam. Margarita took them down and threw them on the floor, where they landed with a whisper. They were so light—so different from the heavy sweaters, coats and trousers others wore. Margarita sat down on the floor and buried her hands in the fabric. Her mother's clothes responded with a lifelike shiver. She lay down and buried her face in them—no smell. Unlike everything else, animate or inanimate, Maria had no smell. The clothes were tender, caressing, but they smelled of nothing. Or maybe nothing smelled like Maria.

Then Margarita tried to put something on; she didn't know exactly what it was. A piece of clothing. She struggled for a while with the dark violet folds. Just when she thought she could glide her arms or her head in it, she realized there was no hole but only new layers of fabric unfolding in different directions. She persisted, slid her legs and arms blunderingly, without being able to put the thing on. Maria's clothes also persisted, slipping off of her body to the ground. Margarita crumpled them furiously, grabbing them with both hands and pouring them over herself like water. They rolled down like streams, spreading when they reached the flat floor.

Suddenly Margarita stopped and looked down. She was standing ankle-deep in a moving, rippling mass. She lifted one foot, then the other—the fabric filled the empty space as soon as it appeared, then it settled back into stillness. Margarita sat down again and started crying, she was not strong enough to fight the clothes. And she couldn't put them back where they came from, either. She sat in the middle of the lake of fabric, her tears trickling down her cheeks and over the cloth. Gradually, she quieted down as something interesting began to draw her attention. The fabric did not absorb her tears; the water drops from her eyes rolled over and disappeared into the folds like translucent pearls. Margarita tried to catch them but they vanished too quickly, without leaving a trace. Then the tears stopped, and Margarita stayed on the floor, gazing absently. Her mother found her still sitting there. She lifted her up without a word and took her out of the room.

Then there was a period when Margarita refused to change her clothes. She would feel great anxiety whenever Maria tried to force her. Her mother let her be. It was painful, Valentin remonstrated, it was unacceptable, but, as with everything in which Maria was involved, the problem reached its own resolution. Margarita stopped paying attention to clothes, she somehow forgot about them. She would put on and take off her clothes again. End of story.

But then something else happened. Margarita saw herself for the first time. Until then she had only felt herself from within, she had learned a thing or two, but somehow one-sidedly, as if under an umbrella hiding half the world from sight.

She began to make up her face, or more precisely, to paint her face. Her face was like a clean porcelain bowl and invited all kinds of painting. She usually stopped after doing one eye. And that's how she went about for a long time—with one eye that was her own, and an eye that wasn't.

Maria was never bothered, Valentin was not happy. What now? His sister was a Cyclops. His sister was a clown. On top of that, she did it well. And sometimes snuck out of the house with only one eye painted like this.

One day it was he who stopped her in the middle of putting on her make-up. He had come to pick her up to visit some friends. She was just finishing one eye. When he dragged her to the taxi, he couldn't say if she had managed to finish with it or if he had interrupted her. Her eye was made-up perfectly, even Valentin couldn't deny it.

Margarita entered their friends' house without the slightest embarrassment. He was walking close by her side and everyone began to turn around. Then a mirror made him stop short in his stride. He and Margarita. He and his sister. The two of them together.

Half of her face was identical to his. As if she had merely borrowed it. For the time being. The other half . . . the other half was something Valentin felt unable to describe. It was the most beautiful thing he had ever seen. Names of stones dashed through his mind—turquoise, sapphire, ruby, gold, malachite, onyx. What else? Nothing. It was something alive looking at him in the mirror. It was like an ephemerally divine gift for infidels. For the wretched. A gift to make them pause, stunned for a second. A handful of time.

A handful of precious stones. Valentin stared at the other face of his sister. The one that was not his own.

Other faces crowded around them. Other voices gathered, saying pleasant things. The din was becoming denser and denser.

The two remained frozen.

Until Margarita pulled herself away and ran out.

## 19.
### Forward and Backward

Margarita often filled her black bag with things and went out.

No one knew where she went. No one knew what she had in that bag. She carried the heavy thing everywhere with her, and like the weight on a pendulum, the bag always brought her home.

One evening Valentin found a laptop in the bag. A magnificent little machine, a real gem. Where could she have gotten it from— had she stolen it? In answer to his questions, at first Margarita calmly repeated that it was hers. Then she flew into a rage and threw something at Valentin. In the end, she grew sad and shut herself up completely.

Valentin insisted and Maria was obliged to go to Margarita's room. When she entered, Margarita was asleep curled on the bed. Maria lifted the object tentatively, as if its weight could provide an explanation. She held it up for a while; too long, Valentin thought.

Then she placed it back, took Valentin's hand and pulled him out of the room.

He could not accept the sudden and inexplicable appearance of this object. Finally, Maria, kindly enough, told him that if Margarita had stolen it, they would be charged with theft and that was it. What was this, some kind of irresponsible accountability? This was his own mother. Margarita didn't just conjure up the damn thing, he screamed at her, slamming the kitchen door and locking himself in his room.

He was angry for several days. When he saw Margarita hanging her bag over her shoulder and leaving again, he decided to follow her, sneaking noiselessly behind her. Margarita changed multiple buses and tramways, most of the time traveling in a circle. Finally she got off and headed with a firm step up the steep boulevard toward the crossing called Krusta. When she reached the top of the hill, she stopped at the traffic lights and stood there for a while. Then turned and headed for Hladilnika.

Valentin was getting annoyed. This was probably useless. For a moment he thought of catching up with his sister and helping her carry the heavy bag. It would have never crossed her mind that he might be following her. He was also getting tired, but now his legs seemed to be doing the walking alone. There was nothing to be done; he had to continue what he had started this morning. He had to follow the mysterious itineraries his sister was walking and protect her from unimaginable dangers.

When Margarita finally reached the first tram stop, he was cursing her for having walked for miles. With astonishment, he saw her climb into an empty tram going in the opposite direction. On the other hand, trams could not go in any other direction from here. She sat down, rummaged through her bag, and, in that long and empty tramcar, took out the computer, opening it on her lap like a first-class traveler on an airplane. Locals and residents from other parts of Sofia were filling the tram, so he hurried to take the seat behind her and look at the screen. No one else was paying attention to what Margarita was doing.

She was playing a rather complex game of solitaire, which looked like Clock Solitaire, but the cards were not arranged in a twelve-point star. At first it seemed that she was moving the cursor randomly across the screen, but then he realized that she was wielding the in-built mouse with impressive skill. And all of a sudden the game was over and she had won. The tramcar, already half-full, started to move.

Before they reached Vazrazhdane, where Margarita prepared to get off, obviously to return home, she had won quite a few games of solitaire, on average a game every couple of stops. He let her descend from the tram alone and stayed on, feeling a kind of dazed relief. Margarita had apparently won her right to go out and play with the computer.

Valentin got off several stops after his sister and also headed home. He was ashamed, but he had managed to get some kind of essential information. He had witnessed something that could serve as an explanation, although he knew it didn't really explain anything. Some words could be used to describe what Margarita was doing with the computer, but so what? Other words could be used to describe what had happened between him and Raya, but so what? Such words could form sentences full of pathos, yet they didn't lead to any clarity or illumination. They couldn't show him a way, or reveal a place where everything resolved itself and fell into place, if not forever, at least for a while. Why could things happen like this, but also like that, and otherwise?

Valentin felt like he had become the embodiment of a crossroads and that there were many possible directions. And he silently cursed his fate—to have been born an imperfect being, and lured, who knows why or how, into searching for meaning.

---

## 20.
## Suite

---

The gentleman with the umbrella entered the café, looked around him for a place to leave his umbrella and after freeing himself of the thing by propping it up against the edge of the table, sat down and stared at it. Suddenly there was the sound of parchment-dry skin, hands rubbing together, and his fingers produced a kind of impatient double snap. He cast a glance around, as if to stretch his neck inside his shirt and jacket, though elegantly enough not to attract any attention. Still, several pairs of bored eyes briefly turned in his direction, then, the movement caused by his entry having subsided, his presence was accepted as a fact. The gentleman rose from his seat a little and settled back comfortably, obviously in a peaceful state of mind. He laughed to himself at the thought of the panicky "No room! There's no room!" from *Alice in Wonderland*, and felt happy.

The place was just the way he liked it—ceilings at least fifteen feet high, lined with plaster friezes, supported by large cream-colored marble columns; a thick, dark-green carpet on the floor and shiny brass ornaments over the heavy, polished furniture; ample,

cushiony armchairs that invited intimacy; a discreet melody drifting from the enormous white grand piano which someone was
probably playing.

In such a place, even waiting could be pleasurable. And he
assumed the posture of a patient guest waiting for his party with
an expression of benevolent tolerance.

He was meeting a client in a divorce case. She had emphati-
cally refused to come to his office, for who knows what complicated reasons. So their first meeting was to take place on neutral
ground, far from the courtroom, over afternoon tea whose taste
could delicately suggest the *beau monde*. He had already ordered
his tea and wondered whether his client would appear before the
waiter returned, and whether his client would be able to recognize
him. The elaborate ritual of recognizing someone, with its "oh"
and "ah" and "are you . . . oh, I recognized you immediately." The
gentleman speculated if their conversation in such circumstances
could be called "tête-à-tête." It probably could, if it came to that.
Some deluded hope that their starting positions would be equal,
a game whose purpose was to distance themselves from what
usually happened and so suppress the mounting anxiety. He felt
satisfaction at his own ability to analyze the situation. Everything
seemed under control.

Two people, a man and a young woman, entered, leaving the
winter afternoon behind them, and sat down at a small table. The
man reached forward and switched on the table lamp, which envel-
oped him and the woman in a golden circle of light. What calm and
somehow objective harmony other people could project. His mother had her own way of making a similar kind of observation—why
couldn't we be like other people and get it right for once? People

were her preferred object of contemplation. And really, what could be more interesting than people, than the perpetual back-and-forth movement of glances from us to them, and from them to us, and the infinite variety of interpretations it engendered. People, the product of our outward looking gaze.

Enough; the silly meanderings of a bored mind. The young woman at the neighboring table was slowly taking her slender hands out of unlined leather gloves, literally peeling them off. The man with her was having a full-fledged conversation with the waiter.

The gentleman finally took his eyes off them and focused on the russet color of his tea. Only then did he realize that he had been staring at these people with admiration: they were very beautiful. Were they always and everywhere so beautiful? Probably not, but what difference did it make, now they were: a tableau on a small stage, and those lucky to be there observed the scene.

His umbrella suddenly came to life, slipping slowly off the table, and fell on the carpet with a thump. The gentleman looked at it languidly, without moving. Then he felt that someone was standing next to his table, someone with a tiny fragile body, cloaked in a mass of hair. An odd-looking woman with a baby in her arms, the unlikely silhouette of an outcast about to extend a begging hand? His fingers were already reaching for his pocket, when he heard "Good evening" from an equally unexpected voice that made him freeze. A lower class, yet educated voice aware of its power over the listener. His professional curiosity was piqued just as he began to realize that this incongruous figure might be the woman he was waiting for. He immediately jumped to his feet and his arms opened in an overly dramatic invitation to sit. Unembarrassed, the woman alighted like a bird on the sofa next to him. He had not yet replied to her greeting when he met her eyes, the color of fog. There was none of the "oh" and "ah" he had imagined, nor any other signs of communication. The woman, having emerged from the numbing cold, sleeping baby in her arms, simply sat next to him as if her place had always been there. Her presence, impossible to reference or classify, transfixed him.

The gentleman grabbed his teacup as if it were a life preserver, and tried to smile.

It wasn't you I spoke to on the phone, was it?

His ability to draw connections between things was slowly coming back.

No, it wasn't.

Her voice embraced him again, annihilating his willingness to speak. She is unreal, he thought unwittingly, such creatures exist only in fairy tales, and fairy tales, too, are unreal. Then a relieving possibility—could she be a gypsy?

He tried to examine her discreetly, which didn't seem very difficult because she was looking straight ahead, with an unhurried expression, as if not expecting anything at all. And what was there to see? Her dark hair shrouded her body so closely that only her face remained open, glowing with an opalescent light, with the baby's head blending into it. There was a supple movement and from her hair emerged pale fingers holding a lit cigarette. The woman drew on the cigarette, breathing in softly, and set her eyes on his.

Oh God, he thought.

You wanted to see me regarding your divorce?

They spoke for about ten minutes, which gave him the opportunity to understand that, thankfully, fate had been merciful and the woman's case was quite simple. If, naturally, one could call these facts simple: she had twenty-year-old twins from a previous marriage; her present husband and father of the baby was about thirty, known as one of the best minds in microbiology; she herself was about forty, owned significant property, and had a prenuptial agreement. The young husband did not contest the divorce, he had already left the house, and she was the one filing the necessary forms.

The gentleman handed her the simplified form used in such cases, the woman hid it somewhere in the rustling folds of her skirt, and said she would send someone to pay the fee. Both she and her husband, of course, would appear in court.

Meanwhile, the gentleman had offered her tea, or perhaps something else, but the woman had ignored both his question and the waiter's expectant pause. There was no contact between her and the overall system that made the café function, as if they were meeting on a cloud, beyond time and space. The gentleman never managed to draw her attention to anything beside the object of their meeting. It was agreed that he would be paid for his services through a bank transfer after the case was closed. The amount of money was never discussed.

Throughout this exchange the baby remained asleep, and refined chatter purled around them but never reached the gentleman's ears. The woman's voice consumed all space, displacing everything else. If she had but wished for anything, he would have rushed to satisfy her, or would have died on the spot. He silently thanked fate again that she had never wanted anything more than an outline of the routine procedures, which he described to her in some sort of semi-automatic trance.

At one point, he caught in his peripheral vision her silhouette standing up by the table. He heard an ineffable "Goodbye," and the creature disappeared as unexpectedly as she had arrived.

The gentleman rubbed his stiff neck and, with some vague feeling of shame, began to regain his senses. The beautiful couple at the neighboring table was still there, but now they didn't seem extraordinary at all. Beauty had become plain and bearable.

---

## 21.
## *Backward*

---

Margarita had not left her room for two days. Prickly cookie crumbs and whole or half-eaten apples were strewn among the sheets on her enormous bed. Piles of clothes carpeted the floor, upon which Margarita's bare feet now softly descended. She could hear indistinguishable noise from the bathroom, whose open door was throwing light into the encroaching darkness of her room. She had reached the state where taking a bath and getting dressed, or going to the kitchen, were becoming possible. The big table lamp from her grandmother attracted her attention and she flipped the switch. The lamp came on, reflecting back eyes from the past, looking. She turned on the tap to fill the bathtub and, with the temerity of an anaesthetized patient, opened the door to the hallway. There was no sound, none whatsoever. She shuffled her feet around a couple of corners and came into the kitchen. No one here, either. Maria, or rather, her mother, no—their mother—was out. Her big blue mug was on the kitchen table, but it was clean, no traces of coffee. Margarita headed for the baby's room. The crib was empty, except for a few toys. It smelled like baby.

Being alone, she relaxed into her typical dazed, free-floating state of mind. There was no need to worry whether she appeared ridiculous. Whether she could frighten someone. She would take her bath at leisure and go out to look for Valentin. Where? Somewhere by the university. Yes, that was what she was going to do.

A little later, her enormous bag on her shoulder, Margarita was scuffling along the little streets by the Czech Club near the university. Her long black coat fluttered behind her like a cloak. She approached a group of people in front of the club, stamping their feet in the cold under the glimmer of the lantern above the door. The place was still very popular and too small to accommodate all who wanted to get in.

Big snowflakes descended slowly through the darkness and melted in the light. Margarita stopped for a while by the group of people, but then suddenly felt hungry. She bought a bar of chocolate, and munching, continued on her way. Cold chocolate under falling snow, the nicest thing. Her bag shifted like a balancing weight on her left shoulder. Why had she taken it, and why was it always so heavy? Her inability to answer these questions drove Valentin to despair. She barely lifted her heels from the pavement now, sliding them instead, like skates on ice. Night's winter in the hushed streets and the scattered flicker of lights. She entered the dark hallway of a building, and not finding an elevator, took the stairs. When she reached the landing one floor below the garret, the lights went off. Her fingers felt their way to a button that turned out to be a bell and not a light switch. A door opened almost instantaneously and Margarita blinked in the dark. She explained that she was going up to the garret. The young man who opened the door stared at her, then pressed the light switch and disappeared. Margarita climbed the stairs and found herself in front of many doors, some of which apparently led to inhabited apartments. She knocked on each one. There was no answer, so she calmly turned around and went down the stairs. Valentin was not there.

She roamed the streets for an hour, twice crossed the Doctor's Garden under tree branches weighed down by snow, climbed another two sets of stairs, rang the bells on several doors to no avail—and finally decided to return home. It was getting colder.

The tramcar was surprisingly warm and full of people. The first face she saw on entering the tram was that of Valentin. He started to make his way toward her, gesturing incomprehensibly and smiling. When he finally reached her, he kissed her in the middle of her blissful face, on her nose.

Where have you been in this freezing cold?

I was looking for you—was her answer, which provoked a nod of despair from Valentin. He explained that he was just about to go home to pick up some books.

Are you carrying rocks? Valentin tried to lift her bag. He knew the question was not going to receive an answer. He simply took the bag off his sister's shoulder and bowed under its weight.

When they entered the apartment, it was still deserted. To their shared, unspoken relief. These moments, when it was just the two of them, were rare.

While Valentin was searching through his room and the bookshelves, Margarita sat down at the table with a small jug of wine and two glasses. After a while, Valentin settled next to her and started talking. Margarita was not listening to him, she was just looking at him blissfully, repeating to herself that she had found him. Where exactly was his garret?—It didn't matter. One day she would find out. He kept chatting, carefully watching the expression on her face. This faraway, happy girl, his own crazy sister, the lovely Margarita. He felt like grabbing her by the shoulders and shaking her awake. But now was not the time. Now he just wanted to look at her and to talk, without getting her involved in anything, letting her be the way she wanted to be. Right in the middle of all kinds of things happening, staring absently.

The floor shook lightly. Valentin looked up and saw the ceiling lamp quiver. He lunged for their coats; books could be heard tumbling in the hallway; he yelled something at Margarita. She didn't stir, but just kept smiling at him. Valentin became angry, grabbed her by the hand and felt her inert body resist. He threatened to leave her alone, they needed to get out because there was an earthquake. Margarita continued to look at him. Infuriated, Valentin slammed the door behind his back and ran downstairs, away from this madhouse where his mother was nowhere to be seen and his sister sat grinning in the kitchen.

By herself now, Margarita began to cry. She walked slowly to her room. The warm light of her grandmother's lamp welcomed her back. She turned on the tap to fill the bathtub again. That was how she drowned her tears—with water.

The transparent liquid absorbed her naked body and her hair floated around her head like a halo. She felt fine. She heard Valentin ring the doorbell, he had probably forgotten his keys and was coming back now that the earthquake had stopped. When the furious bell fell silent, Margarita got out of the water, splashing some on the floor. Her wet feet pattered across the empty space and reached the door, which she opened only to discover that Valentin was nowhere to be seen. She wondered if she had gone out at all today.

## 22.
## *Later*

Later that night, Margarita woke up and looked at the lit lamp by her bed. The light made her feel warm and safe. She stretched her arms and legs in different directions, like a starfish; no matter how far she stretched, the edges of the bed remained beyond the tips of her fingers. The bed is my ship, she often said to herself, my territory, my planet. The planet of the Little Prince. With his sheep. Margarita too had a plush sheep, though it probably lay somewhere, who knows where, under the piles of clothes on the floor.

She decided to take a stroll to the kitchen and, walking into the hallway, saw that the light was on. I must have forgotten to . . . Someone was in the kitchen, someone was sleeping on the wide couch her mother had put there. Margarita guessed immediately—it was Maria. When and how had she reappeared? It never even occurred to her to ask. No one could pose such questions to her mother. A full ashtray on the table and the little bundle with protruding, tiny, child-like feet under the enormous mass of hair. Margarita ran to the baby's room—the baby was fast asleep, cradled in its baby smell. And Maria returned every night, taking the baby from the crib and breastfeeding it, holding it and singing lullabies, and then she'd turn into a swan again and glide down the river.

So now what? Everything seemed to be alright, but Margarita did not feel at ease. Usually things in her life were not alright; to be amiss was in the order of things. Her mother was sleeping soundly, unperturbed—he who can, let him try and wake her. You're smoking too much, you'll turn into a witch, her father used to scold her mother. But I am a witch, Maria would reply.

Margarita took the ashtray and tipped it over the garbage can. A few cigarette butts fell on the floor. She picked them up and then rinsed her fingers at the sink. Water drops spattered over her bare feet. She wondered whether she should cover her mother with a blanket or switch off the light. This way it could all seem real— someone real is truly asleep, in this real night, just like in other people's houses. She didn't dare do either. This fragile being, coiled up like a round bun, should not be disturbed, could not be disturbed. It was one of the first laws Margarita had learned to observe.

No breath could be heard from under the hair. Margarita felt a familiar fear rear its head—was her mother a living thing? A human being? But such a question could not even be formed. Something lay hidden in this tiny, motionless creature, curled-up like an unborn baby on the kitchen sofa, something that no one, under any circumstances, could reveal. Was she sleeping or not, Margarita had no way of knowing. And she had no way of finding out. Was her mother angry, did she feel love—no one ever knew. And no one was ever able to ask her such questions.

Margarita ran back to her room, silently closed the heavy oak door and turned the key in its lock.

Then she lay down on the bed and looked at the lamp.

# 23.
## The Gentleman Mr. V.

The gentleman Mr. V., the lawyer, heard the car door close behind his back with a velvety thump. His chauffeur was going to wait for him, for as long as necessary. He saw the chauffeur light up a cigarette before he entered the apartment building. His wife's daughter lived on the third floor in a seemingly endless apartment resembling an art gallery. With her big cat.

He rang the doorbell twice. Its pleasant lilt could be heard echoing through infinite empty spaces on the other side. Fanny opened the door and without saying a word led him into the living room, where, on a small corbel table, was a steaming pot of tea. Why do I always have tea, the gentleman thought to himself, but he was going to have some tea and with pleasure, as usual. Fanny put the tray on the dinner table and the two of them settled down with some buttered toast, jam and small jugs full of who knows what—probably milk or cream.

Mr. V. had an envelope with money for Fanny, but before giving it to her they had to have a little chat. About this and that and the other. Or the ins and outs. Or the polar bear cubs at the zoo. Or Fanny's gallery and her cat Pavoné.

Fanny looked like a wild thing, of some northern species precious for its gray-white fur. Every time he met with her, Mr. V. went through two emotional stages: first, confusion at the sight of her exquisite pedigree features, and then, confusion again, at the simplified relationship he had with her. Her house was like the Snow Queen's palace—ice-white and empty, the floors smooth like mirrors. Who polished everything here? Or maybe there was no need for polishing, so much did it feel like an ice palace. One could see one's breath in winter.

Mr. V. wondered if her bed was covered in white down, like a snowdrift. Did she go to bed in a gown like Sleeping Beauty?

It was time to show her the bills for the sale of two paintings and a sculpture of indefinable genre. Fanny signed her name in the designated places, and the envelope changed hands. She never asked any questions about her mother, which always put the gentleman ill at ease. But he was strictly professional; besides, he had other meetings to attend to. Fanny was also strictly professional and knew how to get what she wanted. There was no need to waste their time here anymore. Mr. V., however, did deliver his wife's invitation for the weekend. Fanny proffered no answer and led him toward the door. What would happen if she turned now and looked at him with her lynx-like eyes? The end. While climbing down the stairs, his legs tingled with the fainthearted ecstasy of his imagination. So much more powerful and worthwhile than real life, where everyone had to play only his or her part.

## 24.
### Even Further Backward

Valentin was sitting at his small desk under the low slanted ceiling, contemplating the domes of the Alexander Nevsky Cathedral. He wasn't sure he liked the cathedral, which wasn't really a cathedral, although everyone called it that. A memorial temple. A massive church, squat and puffy like braided Easter bread. Nonetheless, a landmark on the peninsula. He wondered: what peninsula, exactly? It was the inland, rather, the continental part of the peninsula. Which meant not on the peninsula.

He was reading about Haussmann's plan for rebuilding Paris. The book was absorbing, but there was also something that deterred his progress. The more he read, it seemed, the denser the text became. He had reached the point where he had to pause after each sentence and read it again, and sometimes reread the preceding sentences. He was moving through the text at a snail's pace; on top of that, he fell into daydreaming so often that he suspected himself of using the book merely as a pretext, or subtext, or transtext—how many more of these could people come up with?

The important thing was that now he was precisely where he wanted to be—in the little garret, as if tailor-made for him. He was feeling as calm as a sleepy kitten, with the little roof over his head, and sitting in front of the beautiful big window, which let his eyes wander above tree tops and chimneys. He was holding the book in his hands, he liked this book, he was going to continue reading it. A distant window beamed bright orange with the rays of the setting sun and Valentin burrowed under the blanket on his bed.

Just then the church bells began to ring, singing, enfolding him in their peals; they burst in, filling the air of his small garret, also pervading that quiet, barely noticeable emptiness that tormented him sometimes at night and which, on such nights, he called simply "my head." What peninsula—there were bells ringing, and that was that.

From the moment he had moved into the small garret, perfectly suitable for his meager needs as a student, and he had surrounded himself with books, Valentin knew that he had made an important step. But was it a step forward or backward? He was old enough not to ask himself such questions. Here, no one tried to melt him like ice on a hot stove and tuck him away in a precious jar. Whatever happened, he could always go back to his garret.

He thought of his father. His father had also found a place, somewhere where he could imagine himself still living. On the other hand, where would Boris go? To some far country, so that he could peer through the distance at his parents' house. Maria had finished with him in about two years, but Boris, he would continue to think of her as his wife. Same as his father. Was there going to be a third? What an absurd question. His mother never changed. It was as if she had come into the world the way she was, ready-made. That was probably how she was going to disappear, too. If such a thing was at all conceivable.

Valentin shivered. The bells had fallen silent. And he was thinking of her death, his mother. Conceivable?

Dozing off already, he realized that he no longer knew what the question was—what was conceivable or not? His mother, or her death? Then he said to himself that the two were one and the same, and fell asleep.

## 25.
## Night Vigils

Margarita tiptoed between tangled legs and arms, tilted lamps, overturned glasses and all kinds of remnants from hours of sitting, smoking, talking and listening to music. She saw a couple kissing, their lips sunk into each other with such riveting force that she could not take her eyes off them. Worn-out desperate things had a strange effect on her. A threadbare blanket, for example, or this hopeless kiss, beautiful like a dead rose's petals dripping with their scent of hysteria. She decided to walk around them, bumped into a sleeping body and the solid surface of an armchair, finally reached an emptier space with enough room for both her feet and managed to steady her step. Where could she have left her coat, her oversized, long black coat and her gigantic bag? They must be here somewhere. The figure of a man holding a candle appeared out of nowhere. Nothing ever happened the way one anticipated it. Come to think of it, even tonight, earlier in the evening, she had tried to explain that she didn't have the time, but it turned out that she did have the time, she had lots of time. And what birthday were they talking about, no one had a birthday. At least she couldn't see anyone who had a birthday.

For the first hour or so, it had been only the three of them—the boy who had brought her and who seemed to know her very well, and the girl she had assumed was the hostess, as she had changed into different clothes at least twice. They had all been sitting around a low coffee table when the girl had stood up and walked away, and just when they had almost forgotten about her, she reappeared wearing something like a transparent nightgown over her naked body. She looked beautiful in the dim light. Then more people came and Margarita lost sight of the girl, only to see her later in a different outfit, which made her doubt for a moment that it was the same person.

Now she was looking for her coat and her bag, and she was starving. Finally she stepped into a room with piles of coats thrown on a bed, and she buried her hands to search for hers. She recognized it by the touch of her fingers, like a blind person, and pulled it out, overcoming the resistance of the soft mass of clothes around it. Her bag was on the floor and she almost tripped over it. She flung it on her shoulder, continuing to tread carefully toward the exit.

Once outside, she could see only machines; there were people, but the people were all inside machines—trams, buses, and cars. She didn't feel like going home, and decided instead to visit her father. The trams' jangle and dazzling threaded lights did not seem inviting, so she headed there on foot, her heavy bag on her shoulder.

Walking gave her the satisfaction of work well done. Work that was pleasant and amusing, squeak-squeak-squeaking feet on the snow. Gliding, slaloming between the parked cars, stopping at traffic lights, standing upright like a soldier.

At night the city looked like a picture. Spaces look indistinct, the houses are surprising. At night the city lets you be; it lets you in, in all of its places, which, you then realize, belong to the city and not to you, a passerby. If you are brave enough, it will let you in even deeper, to places invisible in daylight no matter how hard you look for them. Night people in the city know this, they belong to the city, and that's why they are scary and others are frightened by them.

Margarita was not thinking about these things. She never thought about anything at all. Thinking for her was like floating down a babbling stream, gently propelled by the drift of her unusual perceptions, until someone broke the spell by speaking or asking for something. No one had ever heard Margarita herself ask for anything. If she happened to feel like "asking," what other people would call "asking," she just let her feet take her to a place where whatever she needed simply happened to her. If she ever felt scared by something, she would run away and no one could stop her. She had thus gone through a number of schools, special schools and ordinary ones, she had started many classes and abandoned many, until one day Maria decided that she deserved some peace. Margarita read books, children's stories and other books, she went out with people, to the cinema or elsewhere, but how far her knowledge of things extended was a mystery. She did not seem depressed about not fitting into a normal category, and the doctor, Mr. T., whom she was seeing about once a month, had himself come to a standstill in observing her perpetual state. Valentin would sometimes drag her with him for weekends or holidays with friends, and Margarita would blend in, in her own dazed way. At the same time, she never forgot faces or people in general. Her memory, free as it was from all other things, recorded words, faces, situations—gathering an endlessly abundant material that would make quite a few film directors happy.

Now she strolled about the city and registered no signs of danger. Every once in a while she felt the weight of her bag and moved it to her other shoulder. What was in that bag, only she knew, whatever *to know* meant for Margarita.

The window of her father's apartment gleamed like a beacon. He answered the door almost immediately, dumbfounded to see her. So much so, that for a moment he did not invite her to come in, but let the smell of something burning reach her nose in wafts through the open door.

Are you alright?

Margarita smiled at him happily and he stepped back. He knew that she perceived things differently, but all the same he felt uncomfortable that she could see the remains of his lonely midnight dinner in the black frying pan. He chased away the thought of Maria's ability to prepare something tasty out of anything, her oven turning out unbelievable dishes as if by itself.

Margarita looked at the piano, but her father waved his hand—not now, people are sleeping.

I'm hungry, dad.

Straight away he put a plate and some bread on the table, poured her a soda drink and took a salad out of the fridge. Margarita began to chew heartily, while her father wondered how he could possibly tell her that he was worried about her.

He asked about Valentin, but quickly hit some barrier and concluded that he needed to find out what was happening at his wife's house.

Margarita finished eating, suddenly looking sad. He shouldn't have spoken to her about Valentin. He took a sip of his beer and asked her about the baby. Margarita's reaction was calmer, her mother and the baby were fine. And dear Boris? She hadn't seen him for a while.

Her father felt anxious, the way he did every time he received news from Maria's house. Margarita stirred from her seat like a restless bird before a storm. She wanted to go to bed and her father drove her home. He kissed her goodnight, lightly, as if this was something he did every night.

When she climbed into her enormous boat of a bed, her grandmother's lamp was still lit. She couldn't tell if there was anyone in the house.

## 26.
## Big Things

A tree had to be found, a Christmas tree or a New Year's tree, it didn't matter, a tree to put ornaments on. Valentin was a little worried. The house the tree was meant for was very particular— Fanny lived in it. A fabulous beast of prey in a woman's shape. She had taken him home after a party and here he was—like little Kai in the Snow Queen's palace. Their first kiss had wiped his memory clean and he had lost his tolerance for his family and little Margarita.

And so a Christmas tree had to be found. He remembered he had a garret, but no tree could get in there, a fir branch or two at the most.

He wanted to go to the cinema, but now he was expected to look for a Christmas tree. That was a fact mandated by Fanny. Well, so what, I'll buy the Christmas tree and get out of there. She could have a hundred boys at the snap of her fingers, and a hundred Christmas trees. And a hundred bagpipes playing for her. He burst into laughter and finally remembered where Christmas trees could be found in abundance. He would get Fanny a Christmas tree.

Meanwhile, Margarita was wrapping small presents in gilded paper. Tied with purple ribbons. She put them in her bag without having decided which one was meant for whom. She was at home, lingering like a useless whiff of smoke. To come up with something was nice, but to actually do it was a different story. Having put the presents in her bag, Margarita felt her work was done. She took out a book from the bag and opened it. An action that was like what she had just done, but in reverse. The book was a manual for a software program in English. The idea of a computer had sprung into her head a while ago, and after having carried the book in her bag for a long time, she had decided she needed one. A computer, with all the accessories and navigation devices. Why not, Maria had replied. No one mentioned the small laptop, as if such a thing had never existed.

For Mr. V. it was already the second hour in a board meeting with the directors of the bank. Watching and listening to them was amusing. Everything seemed unreal, pre-Christmas kind of unreal. He loved this time of year—people would say the wildest things and take the bravest decisions, because acting upon them was delayed until after the holidays. Visions about the bank's future flew across the table like comets, circled back and forth; every now and again he wrote down something in his big notebook. Later that evening there was going to be a party for the board members, their wives and several other people with favorable political positions. Mr. V. did not like such parties, but they were mandatory and, as with all things mandatory, he managed very well. He had one worry, however, and couldn't get rid of the feeling that he was forgetting something, something essential, fateful. If such things really existed.

He would never mention anything like this to anyone, not for the world.

Maria put the baby in a basket in the back seat of the car and drove off on the slippery, unevenly frozen road. She enjoyed driving at this time of year. Almost all traffic was gone and she could leave the city quickly. The highway to Plovdiv was clean and dry, and she hit the accelerator. The car was packed, the weight making it adhere to the road even better. Maria could feel the machine, its engine buzzing, the cars on her right seeming almost stationary. She devoured miles, like an unstoppable wind blowing through the landscape. When she entered Plovdiv, it was already getting dark. She knew the road to Boris's parents' village well; she hoped there would be no need to put on snow chains. The back of the car slid when turning every now and then, but it could be kept under control as long as the danger was anticipated. She loved driving, and especially in the winter. She passed through several villages and took turned onto a small, barely visible lane, at the end of which stood a cluster of houses. The last of these, some distance from the rest, was her destination. The headlights illuminated a line of poplars covered in snow. I hope no one comes the other way, Maria said to herself, but just at that moment saw the lights of a car emerging from behind the snowdrifts. She managed to brake smoothly but the car slid sideways and stopped in the middle of the road. The car in front of her had also stopped; a man emerged. Maria stayed where she was. The man approached, walking like a bear, covered in furs.

I'll pull back, there are about thirty yards to the old folks' house, he roared as she opened her window. Will you be able to turn?

Maria nodded and started the engine. The tires wouldn't grab. The car started to shake—it obviously needed a push. Big snow-flakes floated down from the dark sky. The lights of the other car had disappeared behind the bend and now she saw the man walking toward her. She remained behind the wheel, while he went behind her car and literally lifted its back off the ground and placed it parallel to the road. Maria was able to start the car, and after several yards stopped near his jeep by the house. The dim little lamp by the doorway was lit; Maria got out. The bear man stared at her admiringly when she turned toward him. She grabbed his paw with both hands and shook it in gratitude with unexpected force. Then she walked back, took the basket with the baby, and went inside.

## 27.
## Small Matter

Doing any kind of job had its challenges. Where to begin, and how to begin? Valentin unloaded the ten-foot tall Christmas tree in Fanny's living room and rubbed his hands to warm them up. A white box full of ornaments and garlands lay ready by his feet. He lacked only the gentle little fingers willing and able to decorate the tree. But the tree was so pretty and exuded such a sweet scent of resin that he felt it should stay the way it was. Valentin stood motionless for a moment, wistful, wondering if he shouldn't leave. The sound of a phone ringing sent an echo through the ice-cold rooms, and suddenly he thought of calling Margarita. He searched for the machine, realizing that every single room, except the living room, had a phone in it.

Typically, he never called Margarita for the simple reason that she never answered, but his despair at the prospect of decorating the tree alone was so overwhelming that he decided to give it a try. To his great relief, Margarita not only answered the phone, but also noted down the address and said that she would be on her way. Naturally, one never knew with her, but he had no choice except to wait.

Valentin walked through the icy vastness of the apartment. He lingered in the library, furnished like a real English library, countryside mansion-style complete with wood paneling, a fireplace, and shelves with books from floor to ceiling. The fireplace, unused, was bright and clean. No surprise. Fanny appeared somehow incompatible with fire. He climbed a small folding ladder and tried to read the titles on the shelves in front of him. It was a series of medical books in Latin. He wondered how these could have ended up in Fanny's house, and for the first time felt curious about her family. That is, if it was not just money, just for show, as it had seemed to him at first. But maybe there was more to Fanny than one imagined. He walked by the shelves, his hands in his coat pockets. It was too cold to pick up and browse through a book. He admired the leather-bound volumes of Dickens's and Oscar Wilde's complete works. But then he got angry—what was the point of having such treasures in this awful cold? It almost seemed like the cold was artificially maintained by who knows what kind of demonic contraption. He started looking for possible indications of its existence and stumbled upon the kitchen, whose size and whiteness simply dazzled him. On top of everything, the windowpanes were covered with frost. The heavy rectangular table in the middle of the kitchen was the only dark, alien spot. You could stuff chickens and legs of lamb on it, you could cut cabbage, knead dough, and who knows what else. But why did Fanny need this kitchen, where everything sparkled in its pristine condition? Another mystery. And her bedroom, what could it reveal? Were there any traces of life there?

Just then he heard the thin crystalline tone of the doorbell. Someone was coming. Valentin headed for the door, and before opening it to see who it was, he was ready to swear it could not be Margarita. But it was Margarita, without her giant bag.

---

## 28.
## *Other Secrets*

---

The father of the twins, Margarita and Valentin, was a pathologist; back when Maria still talked, she often asked him about his work. Then, somehow imperceptibly, she stopped. The same thing had happened to their relationship—it had disintegrated into thin air before he noticed any of it. He woke up one day realizing that he had become useless to his own wife and children. Anything he set out to do got done before he could finish it. Anything he tried to say—a suggestion, a conclusion of any sort—was already a matter of common knowledge. The children shyly slipped out of his arms whenever he wanted to take them out somewhere. Maria had taken them there already. No one asked him any questions, and when he asked a question, the answer stood obvious before him, or no one seemed to understand what he was saying. Of course, it didn't happen overnight, but the process had been treacherous precisely in its slowness. He hadn't been able to put his finger on anything in particular that he could have tried to change or complain about. Simply whatever he thought of doing was somehow already done.

And whatever he undertook in the house, repainting the walls for instance, an occasion he distinctly remembered, inevitably failed because it had been his initiative.

It was then that he started drinking. No one understood what was happening. Like a desperate man staring down the edge of a precipice, he made scenes. Maria dealt with these in her way, too; could you beat your head against a wall that was continuously retreating? He could no longer recognize the world he lived in. When he screamed through tears that his wife didn't love him, she seemed unable to understand what he meant. When he accused her of wanting to see the end of him, she merely smiled. He asked her repeatedly what she wanted from him, and while asking, he began to believe in his own imaginary answer. He knew that he was instinctively holding onto it as his only chance of survival. But no other answer was offered. He inhabited a world of deaf people, or a world of strangers, isolated like a benign tumor rejected by a body's immune system. He spent an indefinite amount of time in a state of silent torpor, then tried to liven up by going out, with people who were truly trying to help him. But the house with his children and his wife in it was still there—all around him, but also inside him, and he could not reconcile these two contradictory feelings.

When his state evolved into a conviction that someone could read his mind and did everything he himself meant to do, his brother took him to see a psychiatrist. As soon as he said that his wife had taken his place and now lived *his* life, the psychiatrist decided to have him admitted for treatment. The medication calmed him down and dissipated his panicky urge to search for a way out. After long months of conversation and interaction with the hospital staff and the other patients, who were disappearing one after the other, Maria's husband learned two things: first, that it was better to be separated from his wife and children and, second, that for some inexplicable reason, inside him, a problem had engendered itself, and from now on he had to live with it.

## 29.
## *What Will We Do with Each Other*

The gentleman Mr. V. had grown to be inseparable from his name. Everyone called him Mr. V.; everyone was also oblivious to the fact that he sometimes wrote poetry. And he took his pursuit of poetry so seriously that he never talked to anyone about it. His wife was duly informed, of course, but she was the last person on earth to think of spreading this kind of information. She didn't have anything against it. But until he became as good at writing poetry as he was at making money, there was no need to reveal his secret. It was simply a question of self-respect. All the same, there was a tiny problem—money was something you could count and count on, but verse? Who could tell if or when a poem was good? Madame V. was about fifty-seven or fifty-eight years old; she had the heavy build of a German and a healthy look. She inspired unspoken jealousy among her female acquaintances for a variety of reasons: she was the wife of Mr. V.; she was an artist and she managed to sell her paintings; she seemed to know everything and was invited to every party. On top of that, she was obviously under no obligation to accept every invitation. When she didn't go, her husband did, and it had the same effect. The two of them were having a good time and seemed to be a perfect match for each other. He was sophisticated, yet timid, and she was self-assured and sociable, bursting with physical vitality.

It was Christmas Eve and Mr. V. was in torment. Fanny was expected to come, but he knew she wouldn't, and that was a problem. He could almost hear his soul crumpling like parchment with worry, but decided to make one last attempt. The car stopped in front of Fanny's place and he ran up the stairs to the third floor, hoping that his legs would prove faster than his dread. The bells echoed on the other side and the door opened. A handsome dark-haired boy appeared. How strange, he looked familiar. Had he seen him somewhere? Good evening, I'd like to speak to Fanny. The boy walked away and came back to show him in. And there—wonder of wonders! In the middle of the living room shone a magnificent Christmas tree. They kept walking toward the library. And there—Mr. V. could hardly believe his eyes—the open fire was lit, and sitting in front of it was Fanny, disheveled, engaged in conversation with another boy, who looked very much like the first one. No, it wasn't a boy, it was a girl, sitting with her back to the door. Mr. V. froze, but Fanny jumped to her feet, took his hand and pulled him down to the floor by the fire, where the first boy was already comfortably seated. No, not the first boy, the boy. After a few awkward words, Fanny introduced him to the twins and thrust a cup with a warm drink into his hand. Thank goodness, it wasn't tea, or was only half tea—praise be to God for grog. Mr. V. pulled his legs close to his body and stared at the twins. He had a perplexing sensation of déjà-vu. The boy's eyes were alert and solemn, and the girl, the girl had something unfathomable about her that drew him like a magnet. But the strangest of all three was Fanny. There was no trace of her Snow Queen air, her cheeks had a rosy after-skiing kind of glow, she was babbling happily. The fire was crackling to the rhythm of unheard music. Mr.

V. was overcome by a feeling of bliss. Here was oblivion. Outside, the sky was dark already and time galloped on. But here—he was sitting on his behind as if it were the first time he had ever done so, he was sipping his grog, comfortable on the woolen carpet, marveling at the droplets evaporating from the tops of his shoes. At some point other people came in, a noisy crowd that gathered and then dispersed through the house. One could feel their presence. The house was just awakening with life. After his third drink someone propped a soft pillow under his head and Mr. V. dozed off, content by the fire.

## 30.
## *This Is What*

Just when Mr. V. was ascending into the realms of slumber, Maria was spreading a white tablecloth in the house of Boris's parents. She had brought not only groceries, but also a cooked meal for dinner. The old woman, in turn, had baked a loaf of bread and had prepared stewed dried fruit, honey, and pickled vegetables. The old man was holding his grandson and the two of them were babbling joyfully to each other. There had just been a power outage and two gas lamps illuminated the small room, their light joined by the glow of the fire. They sat at the table, on which lay a variety of dishes as was custom. The baby was put in its basket. Maria looked at the tiny old man and woman, as if trying to capture them in the lens of a camera. In their little cottage, with their cat and dog, with their blue eyes and apple-pink cheeks, with their dark clothes and lilting voices. They were like something out of a picture; no, rather, they were a picture, a living one. The grandfather blessed the bread and named each piece as he broke it off—this one for the house, this one for the baby, this one for Boris, and so on, for each one of them.

## 31.
## How Storms Rise

Fanny's kitchen was bustling with life. The spell was lifted from the appliances, pots and pans chittered on the hot stove, cabbage was being chopped on thick wooden boards and sprinkled with paprika, platters were being arranged with pickles and dips, glasses were being passed from hand to hand, drinks were being poured generously. All guests, feeling truly welcome, had an air of devotion, regardless if their work was contributing to the common good. Even Mr. V., gently snoring by the fire, was in a state of perfect happiness.

The music was pounding. Long forgotten lamps along the walls were lit again, their warm rays blending all rooms into one hall of light. Fanny walked back and forth, as if a guest in her own house, incredulous that a turn of fortune could have such dizzying dimensions. It made it seem worthwhile to have hibernated all this time. She felt amazed that the crowd of people could organize itself so efficiently, that the guests were singing and dancing and taking care of each other. She instinctively checked herself: thinking too much could bring back the iciness, so she spun on her heels and started running, waving a bridle of garlands with which someone had adorned her. Near the Christmas tree she saw the girl,

Margarita, who had decorated it. Someone was holding her arm and whispering in her ear. Margarita was peering at a magnificent portrait by Ivan Lazarov as if she were about to dive into it.

The doorbell burst into song again; who was it this time? Someone opened the door before Fanny had time to decide whether to head in its direction. In a few seconds the wave washed a flustered young man to her side. She recognized Mr. V.'s chauffeur. She was confused for a moment—she had completely forgotten Mr. V. The young man's presence suddenly made her remember her mother and the host of laws and obligations that resurfaced every Christmas. Before she could do anything about it, the issue was merrily taken up by half a dozen people. Instead of showing him to the person corresponding to the description of Mr. V., they led the young man to the kitchen. It was too late to stop them. Fanny waved to him from a distance just before he disappeared. It crossed her mind that the chauffeur, who was familiar with the house and knew her well, probably felt like he was dreaming. Tonight, the world was upside down.

## 32.
## And How They Taper Off

Philip, the father of the twins, was pacing back and forth like a panther in his small apartment. Christmas Eve was an especially difficult time for him. Numerous friends had invited him for dinner with their families, but all invitations had been declined with the made-up excuse of an engagement elsewhere. In the week before Christmas, he had tried repeatedly to get in touch with someone at his wife's house, but the phone had rung in vain. Now he was trying to resist the urge to go out, and only the hope of a call from one of the children, or Maria, stopped him. Why the hell hadn't he gotten an answering machine? He knew that, at the end of the day, he would leave the house and bury himself in one of his regular haunts.

He should have accepted one of the invitations, like he had done the year before. But he had decided not to for some unknown reason, and had thus painted himself into a corner. He could not understand why he felt such indomitable rage—which he knew to be the source of his misery. Yet, he was convinced that if he subdued his anger, if he became humble, he would be finished.

He downed another small glass of vodka and continued pacing his kitchen. A distant sound of inconsolable weeping always accompanied him, and after each moment of forgetfulness, Philip returned to his internal restraint, the stake next to which he lay like a chained dog.

Of course, he could "work on himself," as his doctor used to say, words one would expect from a communist youth leader at a high school party meeting. But why work on himself, why try to become other? In order to feel better, was the inevitable answer. At times he felt like he was crawling, squeezing his shoulders through a tunnel too narrow to turn back. It's possible to go back, everyone said, but Philip didn't want to. He wanted to have it all, now and here. He wanted Maria, he wanted his children, he wanted himself with his children and Maria. He could picture himself being with them. Whenever he fell into drunken reveries—the only moments the emptiness around him became animated—he surrendered to such dreams.

He banged the glass on the kitchen counter with sudden determination, grabbed his coat on his way to the door, and rushed to the car waiting faithfully for him downstairs.

## 33.
## Revolution and the Head

Mr. V. stirred and felt that he was barefoot. Pleasant warmth was coming from the fire and he opened one eye. There they were, his pink feet heated by the flames. Someone had taken off his shoes and socks, and Mr. V. realized that he had been sound asleep. The lights were out and the door was closed. He was probably alone in the room. He could hear steps and voices and music on the other side. The smell of delicious things awoke his senses.

His next thought made him jump. Madame, Christmas Eve, and everything else. He gave a snort that sounded like a perfect imitation of a horse, a liberty he took only when he was alone.

But then he noticed that he was not alone. He could feel a presence by the massive desk in the corner. He turned toward the noise and made out a dim shape on the desk. The thing was alive and getting to its feet. A cat, Mr. V. guessed. Pavoné, Fanny's cat, Fanny's notorious, misanthropic cat.

The creature had fixed its glimmering eyes on him and was slowly rising, which made Mr. V. very uneasy. His bare feet stayed where they were, but the yellow irises kept rising and rising above endlessly stretching paws. Good God, that's not Pavoné, but some nightmarish beast a devil has bred for some hellish purpose!

At this moment the clock on the wall struck the hour. The

cat continued to uncoil its body, bigger and bigger with each chime . . .

After what seemed an eternity, Mr. V.'s head filled with silence, the cat stopped growing, and its mouth opened into a gigantic yawn. Fanny came in and wished him Merry Christmas.

Mr. V. braced himself for a battle. He searched around for his socks and his shoes and was very soon surrounded by people laughing and talking excitedly. Everyone was searching, but the socks and shoes were nowhere to be found. Mr. V. remained irrevocably barefoot. Suddenly he realized he was starving.

They led him into the kitchen, where he enjoyed the most revolutionary feast in his life. He was eating ferociously, as if in a struggle to change the entire world order. He threw himself on the innumerable plates and glasses with a force that gathered in itself everything he would have to later explain to Madame. An onlooker would have thought that, instead of taking energy from the food, he was expending great amounts of it by chewing and swallowing, all the time oblivious to his bare feet.

At some point he caught sight of his chauffeur, who was walking with a wet towel around his head and a glass in his hand. The chauffeur smiled apologetically and Mr. V. responded with a shrug of his shoulders. War is war, nothing to be done about that.

---

*34.*

*Kids*

---

Philip settled for one of the crowded bars where he was a regular. He was known by a name different from his real one, like most people in the bar. Girls flew by his table, stopping for a moment or two—Tonny, Rallie, Bunny, Stephie—all of them second and third-year students at the university. They worked as waitresses. Girls from "the countryside" who lived together in a rented apartment in the city, in the neighborhood of Suhata Reka. Their native towns, Radomir, Pavlikeni, and Pleven, were brought together in Suhata Reka by what appeared to be a distortion of geographical space, but the girls dealt with it fearlessly. Philip knew that they juggled their shifts and replaced one another when classes conflicted with their working hours. He knew that they rarely got enough sleep and often starved. That they fought, insulted each other, and thought of separating. Every now and then he would see traces of things he was hesitant to interpret. They called him Doc and would talk to him for hours. Sometimes they told him incredible stories, and he couldn't tell whether the stories were true, or taken from a movie. He knew for a fact, however, that Rallie was a drug addict and he avoided saying anything, afraid to widen the generation gap between them. He felt ashamed for his lack of courage. Once, he brought a female friend to the bar and the girls were delighted. They liked the woman very much and even met with them after work to go to some nightclub together.

He wondered how these kids could live such a life without making a drama out of it. They managed to slip the tragic moments somewhere in between the day's passage into night. They knew everyone and, as far as he was concerned, they seemed to accept his presence as the most natural thing in the world. Philip could not wrap his head around it. They felt for him when he was suffering, but their grief, if that's what it was, resembled weariness more than anything else. Then they would tell him about the most dreadful things without batting an eyelash, and he didn't know whether to believe them or not. And what were they telling their parents? That they were working to pay their way through college, so that the whole family, down to distant cousins, would be proud? Probably all of them had been A-students in their town high schools. Could you call it work, this painful shuttling back and forth between the tables and the bar, wearing tight black skirts, with their little faces white like moonlight? Were these girls the playthings of some inexorable reality, or were they themselves playing, trying out roles to see if they were good for this movie or another? If a disaster was just a matter of time?

Philip turned these questions over and over in his mind like coffee beans in a grinder. At first they would spill with a deafening sound, then they would patter around, lullingly, until ground to a fine powder that covered everything inside. Then the machine would stop turning. Until the next time.

Meanwhile, he kept ordering drinks, knowing that sooner or later he would reach his Rasputin phase, when he would buy a round for everybody and suggest moving on to the next bar.

Why hadn't they gone back home to their parents? All four of them were here, working till five o'clock in the morning. Well, on the other hand, here too were fir branches with tinsel and bells; the snow was shoveled from the sidewalk, the glasses were sliding over the counter, and no one seemed particularly lonely. Rallie moved about like a sleepwalker and burst into laughter from time to time. The other girls were carrying glasses left and right. At one moment, a young woman climbed onto the bar and her shoes flew off toward the tables. People started dancing and clapping. Philip looked around for any of "his" girls and waved his empty glass to Stephie. She brought him another Finlandia vodka, her eyes attentive. The music was blaring in the pulsing reddish light. Smoking and drinking, mere tricks in everyday life, now created a festive orgy of unity.

Then Rallie dropped to the floor and women's voices screamed for a doctor. Philip jumped over some tables, wrapped her in his coat and took her out into the snow, remembering that, luckily, his car was there. As he drove off, he could see the black silhouettes of a group of youngsters. He imagined how, once the car disappeared from sight, they would go back into the bar and continue with their revelry.

Rallie raised her head from the passenger seat next to him, murmured something, and fell back. Philip stopped the car and turned toward her. He could smell urine and felt a surge of panic. For a moment he considered driving her to his place and taking care of her himself. But he started the car and headed for the ER at Pirogov Hospital.

## 35.
## *Home*

Nothing could turn back time. Madame V. wished it wasn't Christmas. She stared at the closed door of the oven, not knowing what to think. She could not remember ever feeling so paralyzed and having to sit there and think. And that was precisely what she believed she was doing. Thinking.

She could not call any friends without losing face, but also, it seemed highly unlikely that her husband would be with any of them. So she called the police and the hospitals. Her last conversation was with a general, an acquaintance, who promised he would investigate the matter personally.

Hungry, she remained seated at the linen-covered table. For the first time in her life she had no idea how to get angry. Her two Yorkshire terriers, hopeful for a bite, ran to her every now and then but she would not budge, crushed under her own weight.

It was the first time she had felt her own weight.

## 36.
### *Tiny Steps*

At Fanny's, the unfrozen house continued to thaw. As if by magic, everyone appeared happy and content, everyone was able to find a comfortable spot where pleasant things happened to them. Even the cat Pavoné had settled in front of the fire, in the place of Mr. V., and was now relishing the heat like only a cat could. The music, the movement of bodies and voices fit together like Lego pieces following instructions by themselves.

Margarita was peering at the people and things around her, gripped by a new feeling she was aware she could never put into words. But she was not worried about this. After all, she and words travelled their journeys separately. She was sitting, pensively sipping her glass of champagne, knowing that this thing here, this evening, this night . . . was all well the way it was. There was no fear, there was no reason to be doing anything different from what was being done. What exactly was being done, Margarita did not know, and she did not care to find out. It wasn't the first time

Valentin had taken her to a friend's party. Margarita remembered all such occasions.

That was why, in fact, she was feeling confused. And the futility of her confusion was about to make her run away, when suddenly something occurred to her.

She looked at a lit candle in front of her. An ordinary white candle burning quietly in the neck of a bottle. Once, they had gone to the sea and celebrated somebody's birthday at the beach. There were dozens of bottles like this, with candles in them, in a row by the water's edge, stuck in the wet sand, which was gradually swallowing them from below. It had felt good, the soft surf, the still, gentle air with no wind, and the row of candles that were diminishing from both ends. The others were swimming in the sea or dancing, the same as they were doing now, or almost.

And the same as she was doing now, Margarita had then sat on the sand, watching. Or almost . . . But the same was not the same anymore. For a while she felt imprisoned in some sort of relationship, some connective tissues, like a fly in a spider's web. That was where her confusion was coming from. She was somehow present in both places at once; she was seeing the same thing separately with each eye. If she blinked, the two images would blend.

Margarita struggled. She did not know what she was struggling against, but it was something and it held her in a kind of cocoon. Valentin was standing about two yards away from her, watching her. What he could see on her face resembled a deep trance, which at first made him worry about the glass in her hand. But she was holding it steadily and seemed to be looking at something beyond the walls of the room. He saw a boy sitting down next to her with the clear intent to start a conversation. The boy even waved his hand in front of her eyes—in vain. Valentin sat down next to the boy on his other side and whispered something to him. The boy turned away from Margarita and burst into laughter.

The candle flames flickered in Margarita's eyes. She felt nauseated and dizzy. She wanted badly to get to the end of it. This here, and that there. Here and there, now and then. She was suspended between two points in time. How long it would last, she would never know.

Suddenly it was over. Valentin saw her get up, apparently back to her senses. She finished her glass and left it on the grand piano. She came up to him, bent her head and whispered in his ear, This here is different.

At that moment Mr. V. approached and, turning to her, asked if they had already met. "No, no, we haven't," Margarita laughed and lifted the lid of the piano. Astonished, Mr. V. watched her sit down on the stool and adjust it to her height. This grand piano had not been opened for years, that was certain. After the first few chords, Mr. V. could tell that the piano was in tune. Maybe because of the cold. Margarita's fingers strolled easily over the keys, and a few chosen people among the present recognized Shubert. And the CD-player was turned off.

---

## 37.
## *Weakness and Breath*

---

Philip was trying to get Rallie out of the car. Finally she got to her feet, but her head immediately dropped on his shoulder. He propped her up with both arms and led her toward the hospital's entrance. Rallie walked with her eyes closed, tripping repeatedly. When they entered the brightly lit corridor, she opened her eyes, squinted for a moment, and froze. Brown benches gaped like holes on both sides. Come on, just a few more steps, Philip whispered, but Rallie stiffened her legs and began to slide onto the floor. Philip held her up and managed to pull both of them onto a bench. Not a soul was anywhere to be seen.

Rallie opened her eyes and quickly shut them again. A marble-blue vein on her temple was visibly pulsing. She turned her face toward his neck as if to huddle in him, and he heard her say: No!

What do you mean "no"? You need help.

No! Rallie shouted, making Philip start in his seat.

He thought that someone would appear now, but nothing of the kind happened.

Please, take me out of here, Rallie sobbed.

Philip did not answer and she began to cry like a small child. Her weeping swelled like some new natural force—it was like nothing he had seen before. Rallie sobbed and hudded into him as if it were the end of the world. Worse still, as if the world had vanished and nothing remained except this weeping little girl who had peed her pants.

Philip felt the sobs rise in his own throat and covered Rallie's head with his hand, pulling her against his shoulder as if trying to hide her. Or to hide himself. He had never been so close to another person.

You're not allowed to sit here, a voice in a white uniform said by his side.

The voice shook him out of the dream he had sunk into together with Rallie.

We'll leave.

Philip lifted the now sleeping girl, took her in his arms, and carried her to the car. He was no longer scared of the substances she had taken, whatever they were.

When he parked in front of his apartment building, he saw that the lights in his place were lit. He locked the car on his side, opened the passenger door and lifted Rallie again. No one saw them.

He put her on his bed, took off both their shoes, made a little tent out of blankets, and wrapped his arms around her. Rallie's breath became regular and soon Philip fell asleep.

---

## 38.
## On the Road

---

Early the next morning, Maria left the house wrapped down to her knees in a black woolen scarf. The baby was still asleep in its basket, and in any case, there was someone to take care of him when he woke up. The old man and the old woman were already awake and moving about, the fire was lit.

Fine snowflakes descended through the air. Maria's car lay dormant under a thick layer of snow, but she never even glanced at it. She walked through the flurry of stars, and her shape soon melted into the whiteness.

She marched up the hill, toward the chapel where Boris had been baptized that hot summer the neighbor's boy had died. Her padded suede boots sank in the snow. The old couple had not tried to talk her out of it; they knew they couldn't. Climbing through the heavy snow was not for everyone, but if Maria had decided to do it, she would, no matter what.

She entered the white forest, the wintry silence. Her feet sank almost to her knees. She soon found out, however, how to exert the least possible effort and started moving much faster. She simply had to lift her knees to her chest as if wading through water. She walked quickly, in tiny steps, like a little black crow hopping in the snow.

A strange narrow path unwound behind her and the snow was beginning to cover it again. It looked intimate and personal, of no use to anyone else.

Having found her rhythm, Maria advanced with the lightness of a bird. The distance grew behind her and she started to laugh. First she smiled, not the eerie smile that made everyone suddenly chilly and silent. Her smile was real, showing a nice row of little white teeth, a child's smile. She walked and smiled, walked and laughed, until she heard her own voice ringing, a sound foreign to her, the voice of Maria walking through the snow. A voice meant for no one. A voice that had nothing to do with the commanding intonations Mr. V. had heard. When she remembered Mr. V. she laughed even louder. She had never met anyone so sweet and funny. He was a man from a family with a history. Or simply a family man. The word "family" made her laugh even more.

What would Mr. V. do without his family history?

As a matter of principle Maria did not permit herself such thoughts. No analyses of any kind. A snapshot was sufficient for her. Analysis made one weak. It interfered with one's goals. People who believed they achieved anything by analyzing the situation deluded themselves. They never achieved what they wanted, instead achieving something else. Who knows what exactly, something they would describe with arbitrary words. Most often, words that simply come to mind. Laughter swept through the white forest, accompanying Maria along the way.

Usually things happen very quickly, just like that. What people fail to understand is that things have already happened. Their senses are only sharp enough to put them on the alert. Those more sensitive can perceive that something or other is beginning. Then they believe themselves clear-sighted and quick because they have been able to see a beginning, or whatever word they choose for it, and they start to think. Laughter rang through the forest, scattering through the snow.

Other people needed to think. Maria simply knew things. Thinking made the years of one's life feel like a burden. But Maria was hopping lightly; her breath came out in laughs, carrying her forward.

Poor man. She never meant to shock him. Or at least not as much. She didn't want to think about him. What a strange thing, she was thinking. He was so funny and so kind, he deserved . . . Who knows really? Maria burst into laughter again and fell in the snow.

She remained lying in the soft thickness. She rolled over on her back and spread her arms. Down there the tree branches were black. Black on white. Or black under white. Or white over black.

And the snow was falling and falling. She imagined closing her eyes and white snowflakes covering her black scarf and her black hair and her black velvety boots.

She felt tempted like never before. The unspeakable tenderness of the snow. Black underneath the white. The world can be described. Maria knew this. Or rather, the world allows descriptions. And resists thought. Maria turned sideways onto her elbow and propped her head on her hand. As if she was on a bed. A bed as wide as a forest. The snow descended like a winding sheet. The world accepts you if you don't try to think about it. Maria was not thinking about it, she was watching it. She was watching the world, and it was watching her. How marvelous. She never thought about other people, but now she suddenly remembered Boris. His word for this was "communication."

She turned again and got up on all fours. She took a few steps like this and started laughing again. She felt the urge to get up and walk.

She raised her head a little like a turtle and saw the chapel in front of her. She was here, and it was there—waiting for her.

Here I come.

She started slowly, her scarf, held between her fingers, trailed behind her. For a moment she stood motionless in front of the chapel. Looking back down the forest, with its black strokes against the white, she considered the path she had walked. It was part of her now, filling her with that familiar onslaught of force.

She touched the door with the bare tips of her fingers, which protruded from the unfinished, black-knit gloves.

She only touched it.

The door recognized her and opened itself.

Then it closed behind her.

# 39.
## *Aldehydes and Ketones*

Christmas morning in the city. Valentin was watching from the window of his garret. The white roofs stretched under him like a rolling sea.

He had sneaked out of Fanny's with excessive politeness, even though the party had been dying down anyway. His last memory of it was Margarita sitting at the piano and her music. It was real music, wholly separate from any possible imperfections of the performance.

That Margarita had gathered enough courage to play in front of an audience was a miracle. It had never happened before. She played at home, he knew she also played at their father's place, but that was all. How many times they had begged her to play. Something had changed.

Valentin could not tell if it was good or bad that Margarita had played the piano. He wanted to believe it was good.

In the same train of thought he remembered Raya and realized that he had neither seen her, nor spoken to her for more than a week.

He grabbed his coat and rushed down the stairs. The telephone booths by the university looked deserted. For a fraction of a second he considered going back home, to Maria's. Her white house, impossible to miss, was only a couple of stops by tram, on the corner of Stambolijski Boulevard and Samuil Street. No, he decided to go there later. Now he wanted to hear Raya's voice.

The little Ralitsa, his five-year-old daughter, answered the phone. He told her he had presents for her and they agreed that he would come over to bring them.

Raya opened the door and Valentin could immediately see that she had been drinking.

Her eyes were shiny, her words tripped over one another. Like a spoiled child, she slurred her syllables and paused after banalities like "of course," "whatever you say," or "okay."

Their daughter was running around the rooms, hugging the plush monsters he had brought her. He managed to understand that Raya was planning to spend New Year's Eve with some girl-friends, and he left, feeling oppressed by the smell of unwashed clothes, the dirty dishes, and the reigning chaos. What a night-mare. What had happened to her house. How much he needed her house the way it was before, how much he needed it now when he no longer wanted anything from her. How much this house could help him, if only she could be happy again.

He left with a sense of hopelessness, thinking that in spite of all her qualities and her mild temper, Raya was never going to find a man for herself.

And that was all he wanted—to know that there was a man to take care of her and the child.

He asked himself why. Why this torment, this riddle. The solu-tion seemed to be just around the corner, sitting like a sphinx, beckoning. It had scared him at the time and he had decided not to deal with it. But the thing was still there, waiting. It didn't seem like it was going anywhere.

What the hell, Valentin thought to himself and suddenly cheered up. Raya needed a man. It was easy. All men are mortal. Socrates is a man. Ergo . . .

# 40.
## *Love Stuff*

Their story seemed unfinished and weaving a pattern of its own. Raya was not showing interest in anything, Valentin was pursuing his studies, their daughter was growing up. But there were two things that resembled knots in the whole affair. One was out in the open—Raya was drinking; the other was hidden—Valentin was unable to make love. This, in a strange way, brought them together, as neither was doing anything with anybody else.

Raya gravitated toward journalism. She hung around radio stations, newspapers; wrote freelance news reports, interviews, reviews of the foreign press. She could speak many languages—French, English, German, Italian. But she neither cared to define herself as having any particular profession, nor wanted to make herself in some way irreplaceable. She had languidly accepted Valentin's attentions, then his lovemaking, then his child. When he had bristled at the news of her pregnancy, she had realized that she was in love. That she could not live without him.

He secretly admired her daring, her charm, which was winning her so many friends. Admired her flexibility in changing from one thing to another. Until he felt the weight of that lightness. And it filled him with inexplicable fury. He blamed himself, but pushed Raya away anyway.

At that moment, Raya was just discovering how much she needed him. But her need made him panic. While these complex states were evolving, no decision could be taken and the baby was born—to everyone's relief.

Maria offered to take them home, both Valentin and Raya. Raya said no, Valentin said no. Raya continued to live with her parents, with the baby. Unsurprisingly, her parents accused Valentin of being irresponsible, he stopped going there and the first few years were a nightmare. Later Raya started working and moved with her daughter to a place of her own. She did something Valentin had dreamt about doing with her, back then when the time had been right.

Every now and then both reassured themselves that all was well, time was passing, things were fine. But whenever they met, the space between them filled with strange ambiguity, a thick cloud annihilating all possibility for shared thrills and desires. When either of them managed to pierce through the cloud, as now with the plush Christmas monsters, both behaved like amateur actors unexpectedly forced into an unfamiliar play. They tried to guess what their lines should be, to keep things from falling completely apart. At least that was what her father thought. And Raya's father was no ordinary man. He was a bigshot. Apart from the fact that he looked like Jeremy Irons, he had the capacity of gathering the world around him and twisting it around his pinky. And the world was happy. Well, such people existed, nothing to be done about that.

Valentin vaguely suspected that Raya's father played a significant role in the whole misunderstanding, even if only in accepting the baby with open arms, as if it were one of his own. He had even heard him say "the children of my children are also my children," with such boundless, yet exclusive generosity. At least that was how Valentin felt about the situation. But he could never talk about it to anyone.

Valentin went back to his room and hurled himself onto the bed, covering his head with a blanket. Something was knocking on the door of his mind, but he had no desire to let it in. His thoughts kept crashing against the same words, "once the decision taken . . ." His daughter's age, the years, like the beginnings of a bridge extending from one side of the river, but with no support, like a floating arch over the water, and every Christmas he was adding to it. But what was he adding? Length? He was just making it more fragile. Did he have any chance of reaching the opposite bank?

You could look at it the other way—the bridge, once built in its entirety, was blown up on the opposite side of the river, so that whatever was left stood hanging on this side, as if by magic, like the bridge in Avignon.

He let the images flow, drifting with them, half-seeing, half-hearing, giving in to the tingling in his stomach, like a child in its cradle, swinging down into an abyss with squeals of delight. One of the last half-formed tendrils of thought he felt before falling asleep was that he needed to write something, to glue some pieces together . . .

He woke up with the image of Raya's face in his dream. He could not remember anything except her face. She had accompanied him to the gates of the waking world as if not allowed to cross over. He sat up in his bed and propped his back against the wall. He could hear the blood pounding in his head. He closed his eyes and tried to descend back into the sensation of his dream and elicit its unarticulated meaning. It held a key to something. But his mind had never been able to roam freely and he soon became angry with the futility of his attempt.

Things can be thought about. Valentin believed that every equation led to a solution. The problem was that he was not very good at math. States of mind such as this indefinite, wandering sensation exhausted him. How strange that all of these things, decided upon a long time ago, kept hovering about, refusing to ebb into the past. His decision to leave Raya, for example.

The past was not at all a quiet background, a foil to his new adventures. There was still something to be done, but what was it—that was the riddle. He suddenly thought of his mother and shivered. What would Maria do in such a case, or rather, what *did* she do? Nothing. The answer was nothing, she did nothing.

On the other hand, he couldn't stand the idea of doing nothing—and wasn't that what it meant to be Valentin? Or at least try to be Valentin?

Then he thought that if Raya got married, maybe he would be able to make love again.

---

## 42.
## *Post*

---

Fanny was as fretful on the inside as her cat was on the outside. The inevitable awakening. Cleaners had been hired over the phone and asked to come and bring the place to its previous state, its only state—one fit for logarithmic functions.

But the reason Fanny was irritated was not the cleaning. For the first time in her life she did not feel like working, she did not feel like dealing with the gallery at all. She went there anyway, sat down in her vast office, wrapped in the silence of Christmas day, and stared blankly at the piles of papers and catalogs. She flipped through her agenda, but everything seemed devoid of interest. She suddenly felt like doing something ordinary people would do—let some stupid guy take her to the cinema, for example. Her system did not include the option of just calling up someone. The "some-ones" simply gathered around her and she gave them directions like a switchman at a railway junction.

Fanny had always had her life organized. If she did not work from six in the morning to ten at night, she feared losing her brilliance. But here she was now, sitting, rotting because of this idiotic hollow day, this "holiday," and no one cared. She had to get a grip on herself, otherwise she risked losing it. In the same train of thought, she remembered something. In her car, she had a bag with everything needed for a short trip, and another bag with accessories for the gym and for swimming. Her credit cards were there, and her passport with a one-year visa for the Euro-pean Union. She picked up the phone and booked a room at Hotel Athene in Athens. A little later, passers-by on the streets of Sofia glared after a BMW, wondering what thick-necked boss was push-ing pedal to the metal this time.

## 43.
## Erotica

Mr. V. unlocked the apartment door and stopped to listen for any noise. Half past eleven, Christmas morning. He was anxious, tense, ready for anything—an attack and a quick retreat. The words he was likely to hear scared him. One couldn't do anything with words. He was less scared by things in the absence of words. He could hold somebody's hand for hours, rub somebody's little feet, change wet towels, and check somebody's blood pressure. He could run to the pharmacy to get something and juice tons of citrus fruit. But words, words were deadly. They paralyzed him; they deprived him of his dignity every time he could hear himself mumble in response to Madame's fiery cannonballs.

The house was quiet like a closed box. Mr. V. went into the living room and saw a row of different-sized bottles neatly arranged on the coffee table. A blanket and a pillow were on the sofa—somebody had slept there. The lights were on.

Suddenly he felt panic—pills! Covered in cold sweat and trembling, he pushed the bedroom door ajar. His wife was lying across the bed, the shutters and the curtains were closed, and it was almost dark inside. He tiptoed toward her. She was breathing. Thank God.

His presence did not wake her. She lay relaxed in her lacy underwear, which stood out dark against her skin. In spite of himself he admired her body, curvy, but well proportioned, and below the belly, that incomparable little mound; looking at it suddenly aroused him. It excited him to see her strong and round legs meet at a triangle that looked tiny in comparison, almost like a child's.

He slowly lay down beside her and put his hand on her stomach. She was still sleeping. He unbuttoned his pants, he could barely stand them anymore. His arousal was so intense that it was becoming painful. He slipped one hand under her waist, and the other under the lace disappearing between her legs. She sighed softly, opened her eyes and closed them again. His fingers sank into the folds of that place he loved so much, drawing him in as if it was the center of the universe. She opened her legs slightly and, through the haze of his excitement, he could feel that she wanted him, that she wanted him more than anything, her desire growing with his. His hand glided under her body and slowly pulled the sheer fabric down from her waist. When he reached the middle of her thighs, he was amazed to see his other hand half hidden between her legs. He bent lower over her and pressed his lips on her belly, holding her up from behind. Desire was now neither "hers" nor "his"; it was simply desire. He climbed over her and penetrated her, slowly and gently, as if opening a flower. He felt her abandoning herself to him, wanting him even more, and he went deeper and there, stood still. Movement was unnecessary. He held her, filled with him. He loosened his arms and pulled her up toward him. Her eyes were still closed. The two of them were half sitting in each other now, as if some craftsman had shaped them as a perfect fit. He reached for her breast. Touching the point of her hard nipple made them both moan with ecstasy, their bodies had become finely tuned instruments, from which they could draw melodies. She opened her eyes when his fingers touched her lips. They looked at each other as if they had never looked at each other before—her eyes were bottomless and his eyes disappeared into hers. There was no anxiety, no worry about anything; there was only this, here, where everything happened as it did. His lips melted into hers forming a masterpiece of a kiss, their fingers wove together and they knew that anything they did would be right. He pressed her against his chest and entered her with more force, with impossible force, and his desire exploded, disintegrating his consciousness into pure gratitude—toward her, toward the world, toward everything that had made his existence possible. He fell asleep in her, in his place, forever his.

---

## 44.
## Whereto

---

When Philip woke up, Rallie was gone. After a momentary pang of fear, he realized he felt exhausted and slumped back onto the pillows. Images from the previous night rushed through his mind. He was certain that if he called the apartment in Suhata Reka, Stephie or one of the other girls would tell him that Rallie had gone to work. And what was he calling about anyway?

What life was this? It seemed to Philip that despair had deluged the world and people were living sub-aquatic lives. He had started to move through his daily obligations more and more like a ghost, like a sleeper through a dream, as if driven by someone's dreadful spell.

His job consisted of finding causes. The causes of death. Only one thing prevented him from succumbing to the anguish of staring at the pale corpses—his students. He was outstanding as a teacher. He was good at it; it was his calling, he knew. After the last crisis, when he had again blamed himself for the death of a "patient," his doctor had recommended finding another job. But Philip decided to keep struggling, or at least to give it another try.

That was when he discovered he enjoyed working with students, with "the kids" as he called them. It wasn't the first time he had read lectures or led laboratory classes. But he had never realized how good he was at it. If teaching anything to his own kids was entirely out of reach, here at least, he could be useful.

Of course, he doggedly clung to that "thing" inside him. And he was grateful to his colleagues for preventing his dismissal throughout this time of abysmal descents into underwater caves.

He knew that he was hanging by a thread. More than anything, he yearned to break free from himself, to flee from something he designated by the harmless word "failure." All words seemed innocent in comparison to the unnamable, that which every now and then hurled into the world a different Philip, with a face familiar to no one. Not to his brother, not to his parents, not to his friends.

Only his doctor recognized these faces as a collection of new personae of sorts. But whether his doctor kept them, or hid them in a file somewhere, whether he found them of any use once Philip had reverted to the familiar Philip, bending over to examine yet another corpse, he had no idea. What he knew with absolute certainty was that even if Maria and the twins could magically return in his life, things would still remain irreparable—this filled him with despair. For a brief moment it had been possible to be happy. For such a brief moment. And it now felt so incongruous with the rest of his life that Philip simply wondered when, if ever, the suffering would be over.

He opened his eyes again and decided to follow the movements of his body, to become dependent on them. Just as a diver was dependent on the movements of his body under water.

He decided to place his trust in a part of himself that was not his head and that—unlike his head—had never betrayed him.

# 45.
## Whence

Fanny was smart and had figured out her options a long time ago—there would be either proud silence, followed by unexpected retreat; or a bubbly, chatty attempt at re-education with the end-goal of caging the specimen. In the first case, the person in question acquired a romantic aura and became the source of suffering. In the second case, he inevitably turned out to be a miserable loser who quickly lost her interest.

In some distant, youthful past she had tried both alternatives, and both had ended with the need to replace the object of love, either immediately or after a period of solitude. When she established beyond doubt that the result was the same either way, she changed her approach. Thus her life became something like a think tank with a mission to discover a winning strategy.

So far her think tank's best product was the icy beauty that projected its competence like an indomitable fortress. Buttressed with moderate additions of wide-ranging consumerist appeal.

But she could still hear the voiceless call of the *bien-être*, reminding her that this was not it. And yet, proud of her trophies, proud of her sophisticated self-made product called "Fanny," Fanny kept going. Anger served her as a battering ram, fear gave her the self-containing rigidity of armor.

When Valentin had entered her field of vision, so young and ridiculous, she had given him three days, a week at most.

For some inexplicable reason, however, he was still around, two months later. He seemed absorbed by problems of his own. She never managed to get a coherent story out of him. Then that girl, his twin, also appeared. And the whole Christmas brouhaha.

Fanny was back from Athens, but the fretful desire for something different was still there. She was sitting in the reception room of her gallery, staring idly.

How was she to find him, that little boy, Valentin, who, on top of everything, bore an idle name suggesting love?

He had left with his sister. Fanny had almost had to throw them out in order to put a stop to their insistent offer to help with the cleaning. Poor things, they imagined that she would clean with her own bare hands.

She couldn't understand why she was unable to get these two creatures out of her mind. They belonged to a world that had no overlap with hers. She had allowed some mix-up to happen, only because, when she had come home that late afternoon on Christmas Eve, she had found brother and sister sitting by a lit fire and a decorated Christmas tree. At first, she had been dumbfounded by their half-entreating suggestion to organize a party. These two disgracefully innocuous creatures had dared think the Snow Queen's palace might be open to guests.

But then something had just switched in her, unnoticed. She only remembered that at some point she did not want to refuse them anything anymore. As if the spirit of Christmas had sent them down to her and they had won her over. How could that have happened?

There had to be some kind of explanation. They were very odd together. They had a strong family resemblance, as all twins, but so much so that you simply couldn't take your eyes off them. Incredibly beautiful, although in an unsophisticated way. Not to her taste. But still, if she could only compare them to something and get rid of their ridiculous spellbinding charm. And surprise, surprise—they looked like elves! Valentin, whom she knew from before, had not made that impression on her when alone. It worked only in combination with his sister.

Fanny was enchanted by the thought, feeling that she could finally be free. She would now be able to go back to her previous life. It wasn't Valentin who intrigued her so. Thank goodness! But this face, half-boy and half-girl, which they shared together. She remembered that they had produced the same effect on Mr. V.

She decided to call at her mother's place and wish her and Mr. V. a happy New Year.

## 46.
## *The Thing One Cannot Do Without*

No one knew where Boris was. He himself made sure to forget where he was, absorbed, as usual, in whatever he was doing. He was sitting and speaking into a Dictaphone, transferring his voice to the tape—a one-way process, in the order of things.

Christmas fireworks crackled outside, but Boris was oblivious to them. No sound or light could reach him. Over time he had mastered his ability to isolate himself completely, as if in a coffin, extinguishing his senses, letting his neurons do their work and communicate on their own. The voice he was recording on the tape could hardly be called his voice. Those who had heard it speak were so few. Apart from that little girl, Margarita. But she was of no importance.

Maria had appeared as the only possible other person in his life. He had recognized her at first sight. He met her in the street, the only place where there was any probability of meeting her, as he did not socialize with people at all. He had stopped short in his stride and turned to follow her. She immediately turned back and he saw her looking at him with her eyes, the color of fog. They were in front of her house and she invited him to come in.

The rest was of no importance. What happened was simply the stuff of fairy tales. In just a few short pages an entire life unfolded. The astonishing thing was that he always imagined something like this would never happen to him. There. He came in and . . . he came out.

Now he was back to where he had always been. And where he would have remained, if it wasn't for that little girl, Margarita, who had fallen asleep in his suitcase.

And if it wasn't for his own voice, which he heard through her ears. But after all, that also would come to be of no importance. Just like everything else.

---

## 47.
## Snow

---

When Maria failed to come back before nightfall, the old couple became worried. The baby was quiet. The old woman prepared milk, according to her own recipe, and the baby liked it very much. Everything was fine with the child, but it was getting dark outside, it was snowing, and they didn't know what to do. There was no such thing as a telephone in the house.

When it became completely dark, the old man put on his fur coat, took a gas lamp and went outside to try and wade his way through the snow to the nearest neighbors. They had a telephone.

Time passed. The baby fell asleep again, the wick of the other gas lamp was visibly coming to its end, and the old woman was bustling about the house, doing her unending chores.

At a certain point the old man came back, covered in snow, and stomped his feet at the threshold. He said that tomorrow, when it was daylight again, they were to send people to look for Maria.

---

48.
## New Year's and Other Kinds of Beginnings

---

During the week between Christmas and New Year's, while Fanny was in Athens, while Philip was struggling to listen to his body and not to his head, while Mr. V. and Madame loved each other, while Raya played hide-and-seek with her daughter, while Boris was away, and while Rallie and her friends were barely surviving, Valentin and Margarita were alone in the house.

It wasn't the first time. Every now and then, Maria would disappear for a few days and they wouldn't know where she was.

When an unfamiliar voice on the phone asked if Maria was at home, Margarita was alone. There followed a long and painful conversation, equally confusing for both parties. Then the phone fell silent for another day.

When it rang again, Valentin recognized the voice of his father. But hardly. Now the voice prohibited contradiction; it demanded.

It insisted that Valentin come to the hospital to see his father immediately, but no mention of this should be made to Margarita.

His father was waiting for him in his office. He was wearing a white uniform. He was sitting behind his desk and his face reminded Valentin of the way his father used to be many years ago. He barely remembered that face any more.

Philip stood up, came to Valentin and put his arms around him. Then he whispered in his ear that his mother was dead.

For a long time Valentin remained seated on a chair in his father's office. Silent. His father's words hung in the air, suspended between them. His first reaction was to keep them there, outside, for a little longer. Something enormous had emerged. Something enormous was here and was refusing to leave. No one could remove it.

Then he remembered the baby. He had never thought about the baby as separate from Maria. What had happened to the baby? The likeliest possibility, even now, seemed to be that his mother had taken him with her.

His father told him that the baby was with Boris's parents. And no one knew where Boris was.

Later, who knows how much later, Valentin said that he wanted to see his mother. With his new face, his father replied that he could see her, but in a place that was not a room and on something that was not a bed.

Valentin understood what he was saying and stood up. The air was so thick that walking through it and breathing were impossible. Valentin could breathe only in short heaves, internally, without taking the air in. He concentrated on trying to make the oxygen inside circulate endlessly.

He was blind to where they were going. He followed only the white blur of his father's back, trying hard not to lose it. This white thing was going to take him to his mother.

They reached a place, some newly created space, where his mother had also come for the first time.

His father opened a lid in the wall and pulled out a bed, which remained suspended in the air. It was at chest height. The two of them stood, one on each side. His father's hands slowly unwrapped something that looked like a swaddle. And Valentin saw her.

He saw her in a way he had never seen her before. He had always known that his mother was different from everyone else. That the degrees of difference between other people were much smaller than those between her and other people.

But now, he saw her the way he could see her only once. She was naked and her body shone like an oval pearl on a bed of black hair. This was not the body of a woman, but that of a child. He could not take his eyes off the body, it was exquisite. He lingered at the slender line of her shoulders as if he could find shelter there before approaching the face. He knew that if he looked at the face, it would all be over.

Then he took a deep breath and looked at her. The air turned his heart over and Valentin felt such acute pain that he thought he was dying. It hurt unbearably, and unbearably, his inaccessible mother was now becoming accessible to the whole world.

Maria and her face, pearl-white and smooth, her impossible face. Not rest, but triumph.

Yet something was missing. Something was different. Her eyes were no longer there. Her eyes were closed.

She lay in her shell. Voiceless, sightless.

Valentin closed his eyes, and something shook him. He could see her looking at him with her foggy irises, smiling at him, telling him to go away.

His father wrapped her back in her swaddle. Valentin turned and left. He heard the bed sliding back into the wall with a bang.

He hurried. He did not want his father to catch up with him.

He wanted to go back to Margarita. Back to where he had something to do, for a long time, an indefinite amount of time. Where the three of them, with the baby, would have to continue living with Maria's absence.

While she was still with them, her absence, which kept everyone at a distance and made her different, used to scare them.

Now, when she was no longer with them, they had to somehow domesticate her absence. Now the three of them had to make it—Maria's life.

And maybe there were other lives to make, too.

## 49.
## *Parents*

In the kitchen, the old couple was sitting by the fire with the baby when Boris came in. He nodded to no one in particular and headed for the baby.

The old man stood up and tried to block his way. Boris pushed him aside with such force that the old man found himself on the ground.

"Maria . . ." the old woman tried to tell him something, but Boris had already grabbed the baby, holding him tight to his chest.

The baby buried its little head in the fold of his neck and rested there. Boris stood still for a moment. His figure loomed gigantic in the house of his tiny old parents, who looked at him with horror, as if he were the goddess Nemesis come to punish them.

They had stopped talking to each other years ago, and did not exchange any words now. After a while Boris sat down with his legs crossed by the fire, the baby still in his arms. The old woman approached, placed a feeding bottle next to him, and retreated. From the corners of the house came creaking, and then all fell silent. Only the wind whistled through the poplars with a monotonous sea-like sound. But the old woman and the old man, having never seen the sea, remained deaf to the waves breaking in the branches.

The old man stood up and approached Boris. He could not stand in front of Boris because of the fire. He was hardly taller than his sitting son. He put his hand on his shoulder.

Boris's body shook at the touch, and continued shaking in silence, until the old man kneeled on the ground and put his small arms around Boris's shoulders, barely able to embrace him.

Boris was weeping for the first time in his life. He wasn't even sure he knew what was happening to him. The whole world was quaking, shaking off some kind of incomprehensible unmemorable dream. Boris saw himself putting the baby on the ground and taking his father in his arms. He heard himself say, "Dad, where is Mom." He could not remember ever having spoken these words before. His father stood up without saying a word and disappeared in turn.

Boris took up the baby again. He was no longer crying. He stood up and looked down at the funny doll's house of a room.

The room where he had grown up. What will we do with each other? This is what.

Boris walked out of the house with the baby in his arms and vanished into the darkness. He did not even take the feeding bottle.

Upstairs, kneeling, the old man and the old woman were praying.

## 50.
## *Fanny*

Fanny walked into her mother's living room, which looked completely changed. It now resembled the cheerful American living room from *Married with Children*. Mr. V jumped to his feet and hurried to hug her. Her mother glowed and radiated sparkles in a radius of at least two yards.

There was something indescribable about the two of them. No guesswork was necessary—they were happy, they were overflowing with joy. Fanny could not believe her eyes.

The elegant Mr. V. and the plump Madame sat down next to each other on the sofa and took each other's hand. Then they fixed contemplative eyes on some improbable sitcom on TV.

Fanny could look around at her leisure. Not a single word about their absence for Christmas. Her vigilant mother was literally on another planet.

She noticed that something was different about the room but for a while could not tell what exactly. Then she saw that the paintings on the walls were replaced by unreal-looking though real enough tapestries in wide crinkled golden frames. A ridiculous woven Diana with a swan. And more than half a dozen others.

Fanny could hardly believe it. At least no one could deny that the tapestries matched perfectly with the dreamy couple on the sofa. And the sitcom, for that matter. Fanny knew style when she saw it and this here was style; foreign to her, but style.

She suddenly felt the need for a drink and went to the liquor cabinet. Her mother didn't even seem to notice. Before, it would have been impossible to take a single step around her mother's house without being closely watched. Let alone go to the liquor cabinet for a drink.

She sat across from them and they raised their glasses to her. Cheers. There was something insane about the situation. Fanny slipped off her shoes and folded her legs on the armchair, which welcomed her as an old friend. She stared at these funny faces— one of them like that of a horse, stiff in a British kind of way, the other—a Viennese oval, with dimples. Both perfect. She gulped her drink with great pleasure and asked what the sitcom was about.

Her mother relaxed her head back into Mr. V.'s elbow and closed her eyes in rapture. Later Fanny was not able to remember what they told her about the sitcom. She only remembered how they were speaking to her and how she wished it would never end.

It felt so strange. After quite a few glasses and toasts for the New Year, Mr. V. ordered a taxi for her.

When she got home, the misanthropic cat Pavoné was purring on the table. Fanny hugged him and walked around the whole apartment, with a bounce in her step.

She decided to rent the place out and find something else for herself. Then she called the twins.

## 51.
## Boris, Philip, the Baby, and the Others

The phone and the doorbell rang almost at the same moment in Maria's house. While Margarita opened the door to Boris and the baby, Valentin picked up the receiver. When Fanny asked him if she could come over, he didn't know what to say. She ended the conversation after he gave her the address. It was two o'clock in the morning.

Margarita did not yet know. Valentin had passed the entire afternoon talking to her, but without being able to reach the point of no return. Talking to Margarita had gradually taken him out of his semi-unconscious state.

When he put down the phone, Valentin went to look for her and found her in her room. The baby was on her bed, and she and Boris were standing on each side of the bed, watching. Valentin came to the foot of the bed—just then the eyes of all three met somewhere at the top of a pyramid, at the base of which lay the baby. While they were looking at one another, they could hear the child's rising, gurgling sounds.

Valentin saw Margarita's pupils widen. He started going through all the things that could seem unusual and troubling to her—it was night, not day, Boris was in the house, the baby was without Maria, and who knew what else. The baby without Maria was probably the most disconcerting. What else? He felt increasing panic at what had to happen, unsure that he would be able to handle it. Boris's posture and face projected something that confused him even more.

At this moment a bell rang and broke the pyramid. Fanny came in, and while he was showing her into the living room, Margarita followed closely at his heels. She had lit up with joy at seeing Fanny. Valentin left them and went back to Boris. He waved to him to come into the kitchen and the two sat down at the table.

Where were they to go from here? They had come so far and now the silence could be broken, or not. Both knew that Maria was dead, but they knew it in a different way. For Valentin this knowledge was so overwhelming that no words could rise to his mouth.

Boris poured himself a glass of mineral water from the fridge and sat back down at the table. The liquid, lens-like, magnified the hand holding it. His other hand reached out and took Valentin's arm. He grabbed him somewhere above the elbow and with such force that Valentin searched for his eyes.

It was a true grip of friendship. While drinking his water, Boris continued to hold his arm and looked him in the eyes.

The doorbell rang again. It was Philip. He came in and sat down with them in the kitchen. Music from Margarita's piano drifted in from the living room. Fanny must have convinced her to play.

Valentin felt the world swirl around him. Something needed to be done, here in this house, but it could not be done. Instead, other things were happening. This music, for example, and the baby in Margarita's room, and the two fathers staring at each other, and his mother, absent. If she could have been here, it would have been different.

Valentin went to see the baby and found Fanny there. He bent toward her and whispered in her ear that his mother was dead, his mother and the mother of Margarita and the baby. Then he took the already sleeping baby to its crib.

He went back to the kitchen and asked Boris and Philip if they wanted to get some rest. Both said no. Margarita was still playing. Valentin suddenly remembered Christmas Eve and the party at Fanny's. He said to himself that there was nothing else to do, at least nothing else for him to do. He stretched out on the sofa in the living room and closed his eyes. Margarita was playing Mozart. Just before falling asleep, he felt Fanny's presence nearby. She sat in an armchair. There were white candles burning everywhere: around the fireplace and the piano, on the table, and everywhere else. People moved around him, covered him with a blanket, and he sank into quiet nothingness.

## 52.
## Awakening

The baby's crying woke Valentin. In one fell swoop, everything he knew came back to him. The baby was screaming furiously, probably starving. Valentin took it in his arms, but the baby continued to cry.

There was some milk powder and fruit flour in the fridge. While reading the ingredients and the instructions on the packages, he rocked the baby in his arms. Where did Maria keep the sterilized feeding bottles? In the sterilizer.

He managed to prepare some food, more or less, and put the bottle in the microwave. After two minutes, the baby was snorting happily, sucking on the bottle.

Probably the diapers needed to be changed.

Once he managed to change them, again more or less success-fully, by using whatever he found in the baby's room, he went to Margarita's room. The door was locked. It had happened before, but now he just couldn't bear it. He pushed and pounded on the door with all his force. And he pushed and pounded until a dishev-eled creature, wearing his own face, opened the door and looked at him with clear eyes. At last.

The others were gone. Valentin went to his room and lay down, this time on his real bed.

He thought that from now on many mornings would be like this. He stretched and turned a little. Now he was finally in his right place, or so it seemed.

## 53.
## Short Days

In the days that followed, things took place and Valentin simply waited for them to end. He knew that these things had to hap-pen once and only once. For example, Maria's funeral, to which everyone came peaceful and calm. Valentin was also peaceful and calm. What was happening now had nothing to do with what had happened to his mother.

Margarita seemed to be feeling the same way. And visibly every-one else, too. Fanny was the only one who looked confused. But this somehow suited her.

Throughout the visits, the comings and goings of people, Fanny took care of the baby. She sometimes stayed with the baby in the house, and sometimes took him with them.

Gradually things quieted down.

Then Valentin decided to go and see Raya. And for some unknown reason he took Margarita with him.

When they arrived at Raya's place, they looked like a delegation on an official mission. Valentin carried presents for his daughter, flowers for Raya, and Margarita carried the baby. The visit resembled an old-fashioned event where the families of the two parties met for the first time. Raya, who knows where she had found any, served them fig jam on small crystal plates, glasses of water, and some liqueur that made her tipsy in no time. But even that could not spoil the afternoon. Raya was surprised and happy to see the little baby, and her daughter was simply ecstatic. Margarita managed to convince them to return the visit the following day.

Philip continued to wear his old face. Nothing more. He continued living in his apartment, but there was no longer anything scary about it. Now he felt comfortable in his independence. For some reason, he no longer felt ashamed before his children, although he still didn't know them as well as he knew the girls in Suhata Reka, or his students. And he was able to move between them all more freely than before.

---

## 54.
## *The Narrow Door*

---

Boris remained a riddle to all of them, however. It was not because they—Margarita, Valentin, Philip, and the others—understood each other better. And they never really thought of Boris as someone they could not fathom. They now simply knew their respective homes and visited each other. On the other hand, no one had ever seen anything that belonged to Boris. No one had gone into the place where Boris lived. With the exception of a few words he had spoken in his official capacity, no one had heard him say anything. And no one had shared any experience with him. Their only connection to him was Maria. Now perhaps the baby, too. Still, no one knew anything about him.

But Boris was just that. If anyone knew what had happened in the chapel on Christmas, he did.

Boris smiled as he remembered Philip fussing about the autopsy, which, of course, a colleague of his had to perform. There were cases like this—one in how many . . .—Boris had no idea. No known cause of death. And yet, there was death. Maria, dead, was proof enough.

What did "Maria, dead" mean? Boris laughed out loud. Maria and Maria's body, were these two one and the same? Boris knew something about her eyes in that chapel that she didn't know herself. He knew the child she had seen, and who had seen her, on the day of his christening.

Back then, when he had entered the dark chapel, the woman had jumped to her feet and rushed to the door. Black folds of cloth and hair had billowed around her like night wind and flapping wings. She had vanished before anyone from the procession had reached the door.

Boris never dared ask if anyone else had seen her. The seeping fog of her eyes had filled his. No one had spoken about her. But he never doubted that she existed. Until the day he met her. On the street, in broad daylight, in the middle of the city. And again, she saw him. And he saw her. Nothing before that encounter had ever held any importance for Boris. He stayed with her, and that was that.

In what world had their meeting taken place? And was there anyone who had witnessed it, could someone speak of it, say anything? For example, how the baby had appeared. Everything between Boris and Maria was lost to memory. It was "something like nothing else," obscuring their meeting in the chapel from view, like a cloud.

With one exception. The girl, Margarita, had heard the story.

When he had found her sleeping in his suitcase and heard, through her ears, his own voice, Boris had felt the urge to destroy the whole thing. Undo. The recording or Margarita, either way. But he was not able to. It was not so simple to lift the suitcase and carry them away. The Suitcase Man.

It was not so simple to leave them either. But still, he did just that. He left them.

Many days later he came back for his suitcase. Margarita begged him to give her the box with the fairy tales. He picked a few tapes at random and gave them to her.

Now when all was coming to an end, Boris tried to imagine the whole picture. Maria, his parents, the baby, Margarita. Everyone was in their place. He had left his son on Margarita's bed. Maybe they were going to listen to the "fairy tales from the box" together. He himself was not in the picture. Just as he had always wanted it to be.

Boris smiled and got up. Just a little more and then it was over.

He headed downhill. He was walking slowly. The snow had again erased all traces. To the narrow door. In order to go back, he thought to himself, I'll need to make a new path.

Albena Stambolova is the author of three novels: *Everything Happens as It Does*, *Hop-Hop the Stars*, and *An Adventure, to Pass the Time*. She has also published a collection of short stories, *Three Dots*, and a psychoanalytical study on Marguerite Duras, *Sickness in Death*. She currently lives in Bulgaria, where she works as a psychological and organizational consultant, and is working on a book about fairy tales.

Olga Nikolova completed her PhD at Harvard University, with a dissertation on modern poetry, graphic design, and academic writing. Disaffected by academic conventions, she redirected her attention to translation. She's been translating the works of Ezra Pound and Gertrude Stein into Bulgarian, and *Everything Happens as It Does* is her first translation into English.

Open Letter—the University of Rochester's nonprofit, literary translation press—is one of only a handful of publishing houses dedicated to increasing access to world literature for English readers. Publishing ten titles in translation each year, Open Letter searches for works that are extraordinary and influential, works that we hope will become the classics of tomorrow.

Making world literature available in English is crucial to opening our cultural borders, and its availability plays a vital role in maintaining a healthy and vibrant book culture. Open Letter strives to cultivate an audience for these works by helping readers discover imaginative, stunning works of fiction and poetry, and by creating a constellation of international writing that is engaging, stimulating, and enduring.

Current and forthcoming titles from Open Letter include works from Argentina, Denmark, France, Germany, Italy, Latvia, Poland, Russia, and many other countries.

www.openletterbooks.org